TORCH LIGHT

James D. Miner

ISBN: 978-1-736718-1-9
Library of Congress Control Number: 2021938784

To the Big Dogs
and
heroes everywhere who answer the bell

CHAPTER ONE

I am Superman.

Every time the bell rings, I jump out of my bunk and, faster than a speeding bullet, I run down the stairs of my firehouse, Engine 39. I pull up my Superman boots, slip on my Superman coat, plop my Superman helmet on my head, and yank the straps tight. With my superhero buddies, I ride a crimson and chrome chariot with sirens blaring, sending out a blur of red and white lights through the black ghetto of Buffalo, New York. Superman pulls people out of burning buildings, clears the throats of toddlers when they tried to swallow their hot dog whole, crawls through smokey hallways with flames licking the ceiling to rescue the pit bull cowering in the closet.

When my shift is over and I have to go out in the world as an African American version of Clark Kent, that's when I run into trouble.

On a cool September night in 1988, I lay in the rack in the bunk room, listening to my best bud Willie snore like a rhinoceros. Without the lights and bells and crackling flames, Superman had too much time to think about the mess he'd made of his life. I heard whispers in the corners, caught a glint in the shadows of my beautiful ex-wife, Cindy. I dwelt on her Bambi eyes, her Cleopatra pose, how she cuddled my daughter, Rae, forehead to forehead, as they giggled back and forth.

And how they were doing it all without me.

The bell rang three times, and I was glad for it. I jumped out of my bunk, took a step, and flinched at the pain that shot down my right leg. I leaned forward to stretch out my hamstring.

"Time to rock and roll," Willie said as he ran past me, buttoning up the front of his shirt.

In a moment, the back of my leg came alive and I followed Willie down the stairs. Our driver, Rich, sat in the front seat with his thick arm hanging out the window. The rig rasped when it started and settled into a rumble so deep I could feel it in my chest. Black smoke spit out of the exhaust. I walked to my locker and opened it to find that familiar beauty smiling at me, sweeping her golden hair to the side with a flick of her fingers, her two points pushing through her tank top and threatening to erupt from the poster. For good luck, I kissed my fingers and set them on Farrah Fawcett's glossy lips, then jumped into my gear.

Al, our little white lieutenant, scampered by. He must have worn his uniform to bed because it was all buttoned properly. The top of his shiny bald head came up to my shoulder.

"Seventeen Donovan," he said. "Do you know where it is?"

Of course I did. We went there about once week. "Turn right, then left at Ferry, then two lights to a quick right," I said.

"You bring the first aid box, Sam," he told me. He grabbed the chrome support bar and pulled himself into the front of the cab.

I jumped inside and shook my head. I've been working here for eight years. I knew when to bring the damn first aid box in and when we didn't need it. I didn't need a sawed-off Napoleon who was good at passing a promotional test coming into the 'hood to tell me how to do my job.

"Your back hurting you, Sam?" Willie had to shout to be heard over the whine of the engine. Creases scored his leather face. He shot me a glance and buttoned up his turn-out coat.

"It's not that. I swear I'm going to punch our officer right in the face," I said.

We lurched out the door. The siren shrieked.

We pulled up to a story-and-a-half house with a crooked porch and a swayback roof. The air brakes hissed. I got out first, followed by Willie. The lieutenant scuttled to keep up.

I tapped on the door and called. "Mrs. Owens? You there?" No answer, so I tested the knob and walked in.

Al snuck up behind me. "Procedure is to wait for police on a forced entry," he said.

The hair on the back of my neck stood. "Calm down, L.T. We've been here before." I walked sideways between the couch covered in papers and the coffee table strewn with old takeout containers. In the dining room, one lamp sitting on an end table provided the dim light. A settee was crammed between the wall and the bedroom doorway. A dim face with rheumy eyes looked up at me.

"How ya doing, Mrs. Owens?"

Her skin was more gray than black. Her sparse white hair stuck up every which way. She was a heavy woman who looked like a mound of sadness that melted into the couch. Her shoulders were thin, but her bottom enveloped one of the cushions.

I bent down to her level. Her jaw trembled as she tried to speak. The corners of her mouth drew up a bit, and she managed to say, "Little Sammy." She raised up a trembling finger and pointed it at my face.

"That's right, Mrs. Owens. You used to come to our church. Remember my mom? She said you made the best sweet potato pie on the east side."

"Oh, Lord in Heaven." Her face still shook, but now she was

2

smiling.

"What can we do for you, Mrs. Owens? You feelin' okay?"

She leaned forward, set her hand on the arm rest, and rocked, trying to push up. "I ... I can't get up."

"We're going to need an ambulance to transfer her to the hospital," Al said. He brought his mic to his mouth. "Engine 39 to Fire dispatch."

You could always count on Al to make things worse. I snatched the mic from his hand. "Stop it, would you?" I told him.

Dispatch called. "Engine 39. What is your message?"

I hit the button. "Assisting the resident. Wait for my update. Over."

To Mrs. Owens I asked, "Where do you want to go?"

"Sam ... help me to the table. My dinner ...."

Willie took one of her arms and I took the other. I made sure I lifted with my legs so I wouldn't hurt my back. We helped her into the kitchen and set her down. Her fingers fumbled over the Styrofoam tray. Willie opened it. Inside was a Meals on Wheels sandwich and fruit salad. I put the plastic fork into her hands, then nodded to Willie. He went to the cupboard and pulled out a can of Ensure, snapped off the cap, and set it in front of her.

"Now, your son'll be home soon, won't he?"

She nodded, brought the drink up to her lips and slurped. "He's a good boy."

We stayed and talked to her and she became more alert.

"We've got to go now," I said. "You just call for us if you need anything."

I was walking out the door when I heard her say, "Say hello to your mother for me."

I wished I could.

I'd made it to the porch when Al called to me. "Sam, wait. We can't just leave her like this."

"What do you propose, L.T.?"

"I mean, the woman can't take care of herself. Shouldn't we call Social Services?"

"And what are they gonna do?"

"I don't know. Take her somewhere."

"They'll put her in a home. She'll be dead in a month."

"But she can fall here ...."

"Al, she lives with her son. He's no damn good. He spends her welfare check. It takes him about three days to drink down all her money. Then he sobers up and takes care of her."

"But that's not right."

"Lot of things aren't right. But this way Mrs. Owens gets to stay in the house she's lived in for forty years."

I walked to the rig. Al called after me. "But this isn't what we're here for."

Some things they just don't teach you in lieutenant school.

***

Rich, aka Big Daddy, suggested we stop at a bakery for peach cobbler. It was almost seven, and shift change was at eight, so we sat around the table, ate our cobbler, drank coffee, and discussed the upcoming football season. Al kept quiet.

Rich ate with gusto. He kept his dome head shaved smooth, and with his barrel chest and protruding belly, he resembled a fire hydrant on steroids.

"Maybe you should go work at a bakery," I said. "Free donuts."

"Maybe you should kiss my Black ass," he said.

"Just save some for the rest of us," I said.

"If you keep nagging me, I'm going to finish this whole thing and lick the pan, too. And how come you don't have a poster of a sister in your locker? You too good for Whitney Houston or something?"

"Farrah brings me luck," I said.

Rich licked his fingers. "Luck? Ain't no way a white actress is gonna have anything to do some brother from the 'hood."

"Oh, you think Whitney Houston is waiting for you to call?"

"You're both fucking dreaming," Willie pronounced. Willie had a way of saying something that always ended the conversation.

Al mumbled about having to do the paperwork, pushed himself up and went upstairs. He usually brooded when I told him what to do, as if he was trying to reconcile the real world of the ghetto with his training at the fire academy and whatever he did in his white boy life. I didn't hate Al. I just didn't want him to hurt anybody. Meaning Rich, Willie, or me.

"You all right, cousin?" Willie asked, parking his bony elbows on the table and leaning towards me. Hard living had made Willie old before his time. His face was lined. His shoulders were slim. But for a worn-out gang banger, he had surprisingly warm, earnest eyes.

"As dark as you are," I said, "you can rent yourself out at Halloween. You know, jump out of the closet and scare the kids."

"How about if I scare you by driving my boot up your ass?" he said. When Willie threatened you, that's how you knew he really cared.

"This is too much male bonding for me," Rich said. He picked up his plate and walked out of the kitchen. With his heavy upper body and his short legs, it always looked like he was waddling.

"You gonna be serious, or you got anymore jokes about the color of my skin?"

"I hear they need a model for the Count Chocula cereal box."

"Screw you then." He started to get out of the chair.

I hadn't wanted to ask him. But I was in trouble. I blurted it out. "I need a thousand dollars."

He plopped back down. He spoke in a low, slow voice. "Damn, Sam. Now? You know I'd do anything for you, cousin, but this ain't a good time."

Willie wasn't exactly flush himself, what with alimony and child support for two kids he never got to see.

I hung my head. "These people ... they aren't the type to wait."

His breath hissed out and he sank into his chair. "Damn."

"I'll get it back to you," I said. "I got something going."

"You always got something going," he said. "Motherfucking Turk, that's what you are."

"But this is for real. I just got to get my dad to sell the church. There's these developers ...."

He reached into his pocket, pulled out a roll with a rubber band around it, and tossed it to me. "Gospel truth, that's all I can get my hands on," he said. "I think there's four twenty there."

I picked it up and slipped it into my pocket. I couldn't look at him. "Thanks, Willie. I'll get it back to you, every penny."

"I ain't gonna hold my breath. Sam, I've told you this before. You gotta get your shit in order. Go make things right with Cindy, go see your daughter."

"Cindy's got issues with me."

"You should have known not to borrow money from the Italians. And lay off the stuff."

I looked up. "What stuff? I smoke a little dope. What's the big deal?"

"Don't play your friends, Sam. I'm not stupid."

"You're preaching," I said. Normally I would have told him off. What right did he, someone who had his own failed marriage and drinking problem, have to lecture me? But you can't snap at the person who just gave you his last dollar.

"Yeah, I'm preaching," he said. "And you ain't listening."

***

My talk with Willie reminded me about one thing: the sparkling light in my life. On the apparatus floor was the wooden booth for the pay phone. I slumped inside, dropped a quarter in the slot, and dialed the number to my old home. I had a fifty-fifty chance of my daughter answering.

I lost.

Cindy had a gift for saying something common in a sarcastic way. "Where you been, Sam?"

"Busy. I was up all night, going on calls. I just wanted to say hi to my daughter."

"You got any money for me?"

"I'm working on it."

"I didn't think so." Cindy dropped the phone and screamed for Rae. I could hear my baby's eager little feet running on the floor.

"Hi, Daddy."

"Hi, Rae."

"Are you going to come and see me today?"

"I had a real busy night. I have to get some rest. Maybe tomorrow."

"Did you save anybody?"

"Well, there was this nice old lady who fell down."

"What did you do?"

"We helped her up."

Rae laughed like chimes in the wind. "You're so smart, Daddy."

"Then this man got hit by a car, so we put bandages on his cuts, and stayed with him until the ambulance took him to the hospital. Somebody was cooking and a pot of hot water fell on their dog."

"Aw. Poor doggie."

"I think it's going to be all right."

She told me about the cartoon she watched that morning, how well she slept, what dreams she had, her plans for the day. "I want to wear makeup. All my friends do and Mommy said I'm too young but I want to look pretty like the girls on TV. Do you think I'm too young?"

"I think you're beautiful just the way you are."

She giggled. "Thank you, Daddy. Mommy said maybe we could start with a little lipstick but only if she helped me put it on."

"You have a good mommy."

She talked on and on, a sweet little tune that made me drift away. Finally she said, "Are you listening, Daddy?"

"I'm sorry, honey. It was such a busy night. I need to get some rest."

"Oh. Okay. Well, I hope you fall right to sleep and you have really nice dreams. You got to get your sleep so you're at your best. Mommy says we need lots of sleep."

"She's right."

"Especially for you. If you're too tired, how are you going to save people?"

***

I left the firehouse at eight am in my Crown Victoria. If there was one thing that made me feel like a worm, it wasn't the accusations by my ex, it wasn't threats from my creditors, it was when I heard my daughter's voice when she told me how wonderful I was.

Under Willie's wing, I had become a damn good firefighter. Why was I such a failure as a father?

The neighborhood surrounding Engine 39 wasn't much. More vacant lots than houses. I passed the empty field where the chain grocery store used to be. There'd been two fires in the abandoned shell already. Weeds and grass pushed through the concrete parking lot.

Koreans now ran the deli on the corner. Security screens covered the windows. A painted sign was nailed over the front door: Soda, Beer, Lotto.

I rode under the train tracks. Tires screeched as a black El Dorado zoomed in front of me. I jammed the breaks.

The doors slammed and three figures walked out. They moved slowly, tugging down on their suits over their thick middles, shrugging their shoulders. I wondered if they had a special school to teach Italians how to be mobsters.

One of them, as big as a walrus, leaned down and tapped on the window. I hit the button, set my elbow on the door, and stuck my head out. "Victor, how's it hanging? I was just going to call you guys."

"I'm glad, Sam," Victor said. His hair was thick and curly. He had a wide face with a nose flattened against it. He was about my height, six-three, and probably outweighed me by eighty pounds. "'Cause I got to say, you're kinda hurting Sal's feelings. He gets real sensitive when guys like you don't pay the money they owe."

"I meant no disrespect. As a matter of fact, I got a little something for you guys." I pulled out the roll of bills from my pocket and handed it to him.

Victor thumbed through it. "This don't even cover this week's vig."

"Victor, I got something big coming. This is all going to be cleared up."

"That's good to hear. 'Cause I got to tell you, you're pushing Sal's buttons. He asked me to tell you, he's disappointed."

"You know me, Victor. I'm not going anywhere. I got my job to think of."

"Oh, I know. We know where you work. We know where you live, and we know where you go. Even where you're going right now."

"I just need some time."

He walked back to his car, turned, and pointed. "You got some time. A little. Make the most of it."

They drove away. I took a deep breath and slumped into my seat. I set my hands on the wheel and noticed they were shaking.

Once I handled this thing with my dad, everything was all going to work out. I just had to keep on juggling the balls in the air a little while longer.

**

My Crown Vic glided down the narrow street. The muffler'd been making this poom-poom sound ever since I hit a pothole last week. Cars lined both sides. I saw a ball bounce twenty feet down and slammed on the breaks. A nappy-headed little fool darted out from between two parked cars, snatched the ball, looked at me like a deer in the headlights, and ran off. Fucking kids.

I pulled into a driveway behind a gold Caddy. The old homestead was a red brick two story with a small porch that fit two chairs where Mom and Dad used to sit. A spruce tree that my father planted on the front lawn when I was a kid now stood taller than the house. I used my key, stepped into the lower hall, and shouted. "Dad. Don't shoot."

He peeked around the door frame. "I know it's you. I heard that damn muffler a block away. Don't they pay you enough to get your car fixed?"

"It's good to see you, too, Dad." I walked up the five steps into the kitchen. Dad used to be a robust five-eleven with thick shoulders and sharp eyes. Now he was scrawny and bent and barely five-six. He toddled through the dining room, clamping his bony hands on to the back of the tall wooden chairs one after the other. The top of his head sported one lonely curly gray hair in a field of glossy brown.

He plopped down in his favorite recliner and waited a minute to catch his breath. His eyes were watery.

I moved a month's stack of newspapers from the couch to the floor and sat across from him.

"You know Mom would have killed you if she saw all this mess."

He waved his hand to the driveway side of the house. "Fella down there, you know, next to the Martins. What's his name? Anyways, he's a widower, too, and he has this lady come in once a month. He left me the number." Dad picked up a stack of notes and coupons that laid on his end table under the lamp. "I know it's here somewhere."

"Dad, you've been looking for that number for three months. Why don't you let me call somebody for you?"

"Can't be too careful, son, letting a stranger in and all."

I let him have a few minutes of small talk, but after running into Sal's guys, I couldn't wait to get down to business. "Did you have a chance to look at the papers I left?"

"Papers?" he turned to the end table and started thumbing through the stack. "Which ones are we talking about?"

"In the legal envelope. The yellow one." I stood up, pulled it out from the bottom, and set it on his lap.

He picked at the clasp over and over. I took it from him, ripped the top, and laid the papers in his lap. He squinted and held them at arm's length.

"You remember what happened to Uncle Glenn," I asked.

"It was a heart attack, wasn't it?"

"No, Dad, he fell in the shower."

"Damn shame. Ten years my junior."

"But remember what happened to his family?"

"Eunice? Christ in Heaven, that lady could talk. I swear one Christmas we had dinner at our house and I picked up a sweet potato and said, Eunice, if you don't take a breath I'm gonna stick this here yam down your throat."

"That was charming, Dad. I was there, remember?"

"Oh, yeah. I guess. We did have some good old family holidays. That's one thing your mother insisted on. God rest her soul."

"Dad, you remember when Uncle Glenn went into the nursing home?"

"Sure I do. The man couldn't walk, but at least they fed him three squares. More than I can say than when he lived at home. Fat-ass Eunice never bothered getting up before noon."

"That's just the thing, Dad. The state took everything. Aunt Eunice had to go live in an apartment. He lost the house, the property down by the lake. Everything he saved from the plant."

"It's a pity how they treat the elderly."

"That's why I need you to sign the papers."

"You better explain it to me again."

"You give me power of attorney. Then I can protect you."

"When did you get to be a goddamned lawyer?"

"For a minister, you sure cuss a lot."

"Reverend Emeritus," he said. "Without your Mom reminding me, everything kind of went to hell." He shuffled through the papers. "What do your sisters have to say?"

"They're out of town. You need somebody here looking after you. If there's an emergency, I can do something quick."

"You know what your mom used to tell me? She said, that boy, my Sam, he's got a good heart. She said she loved all her children through good and bad. But she said you was her special one. She was so proud when you joined the fire department. She said she knew it when you was young, that someday you was gonna be a hero."

I bowed my head and rubbed my eyes. Damn dust.

"'Course I told her you needed a good whooping. Thing was you got so goddamned fast once you became Mr. Football Star, I couldn't catch you anymore."

He squinted at the papers. "I don't see what the big deal is. All I got is the house and a little set aside."

"You still own the church."

"No one's used it in years."

"It's got that big lot. Right near Main Street."

"It's almost ready to fall down on itself."

"You never know. It's close to downtown. It might be worth something. Someday."

He looked up at me. "I don't know what it's worth monetarily speaking. But your Mom and I, well, we loved that old church."

I swallowed. "That's why you don't want to lose it to the government."

He sifted through the papers. "I'll tell you one thing ..."

"What?"

"I can't make out hide nor hair of this stuff without my glasses."

***

I made the turn off my father's street and slammed my fist on the dashboard. Damn. The old preacher sure was stubborn. He had seemed to listen, seemed to understand, then he tossed the papers to the side and said that he had to consult with his brother, Billy. Fucking Uncle Billy who was ninety-three and half deaf.

Then he set his hands on his lap with finality. I pressed him again and he said it was time for his nap.

Damn.

Of course I would always take care of him. But that rotting church wasn't doing anybody any good. Unless I sold it to the developers.

It better happen quickly because Fat Sal wasn't known for his patience.

***

By eleven I was back in my apartment, chilling in my recliner. Five hours until I had to get back to work. There was this little freak who lived down the street. I knew her old man was away during the day. I could invite her over, get high with her, get rowdy. But I hadn't slept much at the firehouse last night. Better to get some rest.

I closed my eyes. Memories swirled through my brain. Old grudges from high school. My father preaching from the pulpit, shaking his fist and pointing that accusing finger at the congregation. Me throwing the winning touchdown in my college years. Farrah Fawcett, twirling her hair with her finger, smiling at me from the door of my locker.

The fire truck tipping over and me flailing my arms as I floated through the air. Then pain, terrible pain.

And Cindy and Rae. The image of the day I left them hung over me like a thunderstorm. Cindy's beautiful face drooped in disappointment and my daughter's was marked with tears as I walked out the front door clutching my suitcase.

I sat up and shook my head. I needed some rest. God helps those who help themselves, my dad would have reminded me. I opened the drawer of the end table and pulled out the old cigar box. I flipped the lid up and fished around with my finger through the small plastic bags of pills, white powder, and grass. Shit, I didn't want to get all fucked up before work. I lit a joint. Before I knew it, I felt like mush that oozed into the cushions.

CHAPTER TWO

At five p.m., after setting my fire gear on the rig and checking my air tank, I took my spot at the kitchen table, nursed my coffee, and read the sports page.

"You gonna hog the local news?" Rich said to Willie.

"Doing the crossword puzzle like I do every day," Willie said, holding the paper at arms' length, looking through the glasses that sat on the end of his nose.

"Just don't cut out the coupons this time," Rich said.

"What's a six-letter word for ruler of a castle?" Willie said.

"Blacula," I said.

"The Dark Knight," Rich said.

Willie nodded. "Ah-huh. Keep it up and I'm gonna show you two a new word for kick your ass."

The lieutenant pattered into the room, like an elf in uniform, and stopped at the head of the table. He held a sheet of paper in front of him and bobbed up on his toes. "Okay, guys. This is important. I just talked to the chief."

I cringed. I had a lot of stuff on my mind and I wasn't in the mood to listen to Al play at being a real officer.

"If he comes over for dinner," Rich said, "I'm eating pizza in the basement."

"Did you tell Chief McGowan that I love him?" I said.

Willie pushed the paper down to the table. "Stop fucking around." He shot Rich and I a look. Then to Al, he said, "Go on, L.T."

"Okay." Al looked down at the paper. "All members are to use caution when approaching hazardous material incidents that present unusual dangers."

"Profound," I said.

"Stop showing off that you went to college," Willie said. "The L.T. is talking about the call Engine 17 had last night."

"What call?"

Al read off the paper. "Engine 17 responded to a call at the Central Park Plaza. When investigating, they found a one-hundred-foot trench cut into the concrete. Inside was an unknown combustible substance."

"The green flame?" Willie said.

"You been hitting the cheap bourbon, Willie?" I said.

"No, it's true," Al said. "Something burned bright green."

"Engine 17 had the call. The guys said it sparkled," Willie said.

"So what the hell was it?" I asked.

Al looked down at the paper. "Under investigation," he said. "But if confronted with such an incident, wear protective clothing and keep at a distance of fifty yards."

"Is it explosive," I asked. "Radioactive? Fifty yards doesn't seem like much."

"Well, we'll have to keep with protocol," Al said.

Rich stretched in the chair and waved his hand like a second grader.

"Did you want to say something, Rich?" Al said.

"So it might explode and maybe it's radioactive?"

"Under investigation," Al said.

"I just have one question," Rich said. "Do you reeeeh-uhly believe that we are going to sit there fifty yards away when this shit could be agent orange or a hunk of plutonium?"

"It's green," Al said.

"Green, orange, purple, I don't care. 'Cause when I see it, I'm running in the opposite direction and getting on the Main Street bus."

Al got a blank look on his face and stuttered. Didn't the guy have any sense of humor? But in making a joke, Rich spoke the truth. All things being equal, Al was the weak link in a strong chain. When Al tried to boss us around, like he knew what he was doing, that was when problems started.

But I had bigger things to deal with. I had to get my dad to give me power of attorney so I could close this deal with the realtors. They threatened to go through the city and have the property condemned. So far that was a bluff. It would take some trouble and expense to have church property stolen from its rightful owner by eminent domain. But no telling what would happen if I didn't get this thing done.

A while later, Willie and I sat next to each other in our recliners. There was some game show on that I paid no attention to. I heard a knock on the back door. I didn't feel like moving. Willie sat stoically in his recliner, the television lighting the contours of his black face.

"Hey, Dark Shadow, you wanna get it this time?" I said.

"You know it ain't for me."

"Let them knock, then," I said. "I ain't moving."

Willy grunted as he pushed himself up. He slid his feet into his slippers and shuffled over the floor.

"Could be supply with a delivery," I said.

"Could be one of your girlfriends," Willie said. He moved slump-shouldered out of the kitchen and through the hall.

I listened to the door open. "Hey, darling. Cindy, how ya doing?

Rae-Rae, you are getting so big."

"Hi, Uncle Willie," Rae said.

I shook my head. When it rains, it pours. I got up and walked to the kitchen table.

Rae's flip-flops slapped the floor. She whipped around the table and jumped into my arms. "Daddy!"

One bright spot in the entire miserable day.

"Hey, sweetie. You look so pretty," I said.

Her tiny finger flicked my silver collar badges. "These are shiny," she said. "Silver on blue. You are so handsome, Daddy."

"And you're the prettiest girl in the world." I kissed her forehead. Her hair was stretched back straight and ended up in a puff ball in the back of her head. Cindy always took good care of her. I was grateful for that.

Rae chattered on about little girl stuff. Cindy stood across the table, her arms wrapped around her purse which she pressed against her chest. As angry as she was and as hard as I was trying to avoid her, she always made me smile.

"I wish you would have called," I said.

"I bet you do. Then you could sneak out before I got here." She plopped her purse on the table.

"It ain't like that, Cindy. We just had this run-in with the new chief. He got bent out of shape cause one of the guys brought a girl into the firehouse."

"I'm not just a girl. I'm the mother of your child." She held her head high and stuck out her chin. Motherhood had added a little something to her hips. Her breast were too big for a woman that thin. She tilted her head back. Her face naturally sloped from forehead to nose to a mouth that pouted proudly. Her complexion was bronze. I used to kid her that she looked like Cleopatra. But right now, an angry Egyptian monarch was the last thing I needed.

"Of course you are, Cindy. You'll always be special."

"I didn't bring my boots so please keep the bullshit to a minimum."

Rae kept her head down and fiddled with my buttons. I petted the back of her head. Little goose bumps poked up on her neck.

"It's not the time, Cindy," I said, gesturing with my head down at our daughter.

"Oh, it's the time. You and I are going to have a talk."

"Hey, Rae-Rae. How about if Uncle Willie shows you the firetruck? If you're a good girl, I'll even let you blow the horn. Would you like that?"

He tucked his hands under her arms, raised her up, and clutched her to his side. Her arm rested around his neck.

"You ever go into a real fire, Uncle Willie?"

"Me and your daddy go into them all the time."

Cindy and I were alone. She glared at me.

"Would you sit down?" I asked.

"No. I won't. You fucked me, Sam."

"Aw, don't be like that."

"You got me to sign off on support. You said it would be better that way, that you could do more for me if you didn't have a child support payment record on your paycheck."

"Baby, when I got extra cash, you're the first to know about it."

"You haven't brought me nothing in three weeks."

"It's just been real busy, that's all."

"That's three weeks Rae hasn't seen you. It's not like we live that far. You could have stopped by. Don't you even care about your daughter?"

The truth was I felt like a dog every time I showed up empty handed. "I'm sorry."

"I might get a job offer. But it won't work out if I don't have a car I can rely on, or money to send Rae to a good daycare."

"You got to believe I'm trying."

"You know what my friends are saying? Go on the welfare. I'm already getting food stamps."

"That's what public assistance is for, times like this."

"I'm six credits short of my masters. I had a three-point-eight GPA when you knocked me up. I should be working in one of those big business towers downtown. I am not going on no fucking welfare."

Argument and recrimination, that's all that was left of our relationship. That and our daughter. I wanted to take the words back as soon as they left my lips. "You were the one who wanted the divorce."

"Oh, don't you go there. I won't be your fool, Sam. I already lost a brother to drugs. I wasn't going to watch you kill yourself."

I leaned over and rested my knuckles on the table. "A car hit the firetruck. I got thrown thirty feet in the air, damn it. Don't you remember?" We had done this so many times before and it always ended at a dead end. But when I got angry ….

"I remember," she said. "I stood by you at the hospital. I rubbed your back, I waited on you like a nurse."

"You left!" I pounded my fist on the table.

"Two years after you recovered, you were still doing the junk. And not just what the doctors prescribed."

"I was in pain." Every morning when I woke up, every time I turned wrong or took a clumsy step.

"What about the hoes? Did they make your back feel better? What about gambling away our rent? What about ... I don't want to do this again, Sam. I want my money."

"Don't worry about it."

"I want you to act like a father to Rae."

I knew I shouldn't say anything else because my blood boiled and whatever I said would just be mean.

Gratefully, I heard the alarm bell ring. Willie ran back into the kitchen holding Rae and handed her off to Cindy. He kissed Cindy, then Rae, on the cheek. "Gotta go," he said.

"I know how to let myself out," Cindy said.

You could tell when a call was something serious. Dispatch held on to the tones longer, left longer pauses between them. The dispatcher declared the facts in a direct, almost threatening way.

"Alarm of Fire, 22 Purdy, between East Parade and Fillmore Ave." The names of the companies responding rattled out. Then he said, "Heavy smoke on the second floor, reports of people trapped."

Feet clomped down the steps. We ran to our spots on the rig. Rich jumped into the cab and hit the starter. The rig rasped and sputtered and settled into a chesty rattle. I gave Farrah a little pat, slipped into my boots, threw my coat over my shoulder. I called to Rich, "Go down Kehr Street and take the third right."

"I got it," he yelled back.

The rig lurched out of the firehouse and turned. The old Mack truck hesitated and the gears groaned at every intersection. We'd driven two blocks when I smelled the smoke.

"Rock and roll time, Sam," Willie said.

"Engine 17 might beat us there," I shouted to him over the engine noise. "There's a hydrant on the corner. Help Rich hook up."

We passed the street and plunged into a cloud of smoke. Me and the L.T. got off at the fire. Rich and Willie dropped a hose line and rode down the street to hook up to a hydrant.

Al walked over to me and pulled tight the straps on his face piece. I headed up the driveway. Gouts of smoke curled out of the second-floor windows, billowing up until they settled over the roof. Red and orange peeked behind the glass of the first-floor windows. Fire crackled. A gunshot-like snap ricocheted through the air.

One line already snaked through the driveway and trailed up the backstairs. I nodded to Al and we grabbed another line to back them up. I took the nozzle, and Al followed close behind. We made it as far as the porch when I felt a tug on my sleeve. I turned to see a middle-aged lady, her hair bound up in a do-wrap, a hand at her throat cinching her housecoat closed.

"Ma'am, we got no time—"

"The baby's in there," she said. The fire and lights played a red horror show over her face.

"You sure?"

"Not for certain. Sometimes she leaves him with her sister. She ain't been home all evening. But it's possible."

"How old?"

"George is seven."

"Upstairs?"

She nodded.

I yanked the line forward. Damn. Fucking hypes. So involved in drugs they ignore their own kids.

George was the same age as Rae.

"Come on, L.T.," I said. We made it past the second-floor kitchen windows. I could still see the drapes and the kitchen chandelier, so the fire hadn't banked down that far. That was good. Maybe there was a chance. At the rear door, Al and I hunkered down and checked our masks. I heard a hiss when I cranked the valve on my tank and felt cold air swish across my face. I grabbed a fold of hose and shot headlong into the dark stairway. I should have reminded myself not to turn suddenly to the right, not to knock into anything, to protect my back. But my adrenaline set my body on high alert and my heart pumped madly. It was time for battle.

I wished I had Willie by my side.

At the first-floor landing, I stopped and looked back. Our hose stiffened as water ran through. The nozzle reared and I held it tight.

We pushed on into heavy smoke at the landing between the first and second floor. Outside, we heard the crack of glass as crews from the ladder companies cleared out the windows.

I heard a thud from the water of Engine 17's hose line. Now that the windows were opened, the smoke cleared out to the level of my head.

I bent over and shouted into Al's ear. "Come on, L.T."

If little George was up there, he didn't have much time.

You never knew if it was true when a civilian said a person was trapped. Odds were ten to one against. But you had to take that bet when a child's life was at stake.

At the landing, my foot twisted off the hose line and I felt the old twang in my back. I shifted my hips quickly to relieve the pain and dropped to all fours to crawl up the stairs.

We made it to the second-floor landing. The boots and rump of a firefighter blocked the door. A flutter of flame snuck under the archway that separated the kitchen from the dining room and rolled over the ceiling. Engine 17's stream thumped against it.

I moved up, forcing my way next to the nozzle-man and yelled in his ear, "Make way. We got another line."

"There's no room, Sam," he shouted back.

It was Captain Sikes, a guy with twenty-five years' experience and a thousand fires behind him. The bell of his tank rang, telling him he was almost out of air. His nozzle-man played their stream against the top of the doorway between the kitchen and dining room. The fire lapped forward. The stream pushed back. The fire was winning.

"Your bell's ringing, Cap," I shouted in his ear. He'd be out of air in five minutes.

"I'll stay until the chief relieves me," he said.

"I want to get past you. Search the bedrooms."

"Wait for the rescue unit."

"No time for that."

"Fuck that, Sam," he said. Through his mask I could make out his face, wrinkled and serious. "No one could survive in there." He gestured forward. There was only a half a foot of clear air between smoke and carpet.

"I got to try," I said.

"Fucking hardhead," he said. "Make it quick. I'll cover you with our line."

I looked behind me for Al. The line laid on the linoleum, the nozzle on its side, water leaking from the coupling.

Al was gone.

The motherfucker had bolted.

I could be pissed off later. Right now I needed to do a search. I lurched ahead and crawled on all fours. Engine 17's hose sent a sheet of water upward, scattering the smoke and disrupting the fire on the ceiling. The fire retreated back, curled around, and attacked on the sides.

I crawled ahead a few feet. I could only see if I ducked my head under the blanket of smoke. My shoulder thumped against something. I reached up. Ran my hand over it. A chair. I shoved it to the side.

I pushed on, my knees and hands in two inches of hot water. My bunker pants were soaked and weighed me down. All I could see was a gray fog. I felt the wall with my hand, patting every couple feet. I came to an opening. Bending below the level of smoke, I was able to make out a bed.

I had been to hundreds of fires, but something happened that stopped me dead. My mask lit up with a flash as if somebody turned a spotlight on me.

I had known firefighters to get light-headed at fires, or maybe panic, and even jump out a window. It could be explained away by the burst of hormones, heat exhaustion, even fear. But this was different. The green flash felt cool and soothing. It disappeared and I was certain that

George was not in this bedroom.

Okay. It wouldn't be the first time I acted on a hunch. I passed the doorway, feeling for the wall on the other side of it. My helmet clanged against an end table. I grabbed a leg and tossed it away. My ears tingle from the heat. My breath came in big gulps. If I didn't stay calm, I'd go through my air too fast.

But George might be cringing in the corner. Right now Cindy was putting Rae to bed. My daughter would be cuddling her teddy bear, softly snoring, the covers pulled up to her neck.

I pushed forward while patting the wall to the right. I fought it but my muscles tightened. My adrenaline surged. Blinded by smoke, I went too far and lost the wall. I stretched my arms right then left, trying to find something to orient myself. The sound of the hose line seemed far away. I fought the urge to tear off my mask, turn, and run for the door; that would just give the guys another body to pull out. One breath of this poison air and I was done.

I saw the flash again, this time a slow-moving bolt that snaked over the floor. I knew it was crazy, but I followed it, scampering like a crab. I rammed into something solid. Rubbing my hands over it, I knew it was a door frame. Smoke took away my view of the room, but the green light skidded right and I crab crawled after it.

Fire distorts time. Working inside a burning building stretches seconds into hours. All I knew was if I didn't find George soon, there was no chance of him making it.

I followed the wall until I found something soft. A pile of clothes. I slogged through. Something snapped under my knee. Plastic. Maybe part of a toy. Was this George's room?

The bell on my tank rang. I had five minutes of air left, maybe less, at the rate I was sucking it down. I kept on, patting the wall with my right hand. A closet. Kids sometimes crawled in them for safety. I threw out shoes. More toys. I reached deep into the corner and pulled out old boxes.

No George.

The bell on my tank worked by air pressure. As the air ran lower, the bell slowed down to a tiny cackle. It told me my opportunity was down to a couple hundred seconds.

I kept searching to my right until I turned a corner. I knocked into a shelf. Then I felt the windowsill.

If I was going to find George quickly, I had to be able to see. If I broke the window, I'd clear out the room. But that would draw the fire from the dining room.

I might gain a few seconds. And that might be enough.

My ears and neck burned when I got up. I smashed through the glass with my fists, yanked out the sash, and threw it into the yard below. Now that the window was open fully, air rushed out and the bottom half of the room cleared.

And from the dining room, now that it had a new route to fresh air, fire crawled over the top of the door frame and lapped over the bedroom ceiling.

I saw the bed, the covers balled up. I patted it down, threw off the bed clothes.

Where are you baby?

I fought against frustration. I leaned over, grabbed the frame of the bed and heaved it aside. Please, God.

Under the bed I saw a bundle. I reached down and pulled away a blanket. His knees were pulled up to his chest. There were little sneakers on his feet. His head was tucked for safety into the stomach of his teddy bear.

I grabbed him with one hand and held him under my arm, forcing myself to stay low to keep George away from the super-heated smoke when what I wanted to do was stand up and run. Standard procedure was to drag him behind me, but I couldn't bear to drop him into the hot water. Fire licked down in hungry tongues, roaring out the window, sucking in oxygen, swelling down, cackling at me, snapping for George.

I made it to the bedroom door. A shower of scalding water drenched my back. Must have been the stream ricocheting off the ceiling. The droplets slammed against my helmet like ball-peen hammers. George hung loosely and I tugged him against my body. He didn't need to slam his head into a doorframe or overturned chair.

With no free hand to feel, I pushed forward by instinct, trying to follow the trajectory of the water. Each breath came harder.

The seal on my face mask collapsed as I drew in a breath.

My tank was empty.

I didn't know if I were going straight or in a circle. There was no way to tell unless I ran into a wall or suddenly could see.

Again I saw the green light. Desperately I followed it. My last gasp of air came out like a weak moan.

With what was left of my strength, I stood up and charged in the direction of the green light. I heard voices and felt hands on my shoulder, and I tumbled into the kitchen. There was red and yellow flashing light from the open windows. I tore off my mask and gasped. My chest felt like it was going to explode, but I ran out of the kitchen and slid on my butt over the hose line that snaked down the stairs. People called for me, hands kept me up and tried to pry George out of my gasp. I shrugged them off and ran out the back door, halfway up the driveway where I fell to my knees.

20

I sloughed off my mask.

George rested so peacefully, cradled in the crook of my arm. His head fell backwards, stretching his neck, leaving his mouth open in a heart shaped pout. He wasn't burned but his skin was gray. He was so frail, so small, compared to Rae. His body seemed all bones and belly.

I brought my hand behind his head and said a prayer with every breath, pinching his nose, sealing his mouth with my lips, trying not to hyperventilate when I picked my head up, watching his little chest, stopping after it rose gently so I wouldn't blow his lungs apart.

Come back, baby, please come back.

Under the awful sour smoke from his lungs, I tasted something wonderfully childlike and sweet as if he had drunk juice before he went to bed.

Hands were on me; voices called, but I ignored them. Finally the paramedics knelt down next to me with their red box which carried everything needed to make a hopeless effort. They slid George away from me. His hand dragged over my arm. I wanted him to grab my sleeve. I wanted to hear him cry even if it was the saddest painful child cry. I saw them work on him, cut away his smudged Star Wars T-shirt. They were all over him with tubes and probes. I slumped against the stone foundation of the neighboring house and stared up through the smoke that puffed out of the second-floor windows and obscured the night.

Captain Sikes bent down next to me and set his hand on my knee. "You okay, Carver?"

"I just need to catch my breath, Cap."

Soon I heard them trotting away, taking George to the ambulance, but I couldn't look. I got a "Good job, Sam," from a passing firefighter. Men pulled hose out of the building. Smoke puffed out hard from the eaves and lit up when it mixed with the air.

Chief McGowan walked past me, his short legs skipping over the ground. He turned my way quickly. "Get the hell out of there, Carver. We're pulling out. Building is lost. It's all surround and drown from here." I waved my hand to him and he was gone.

Boots splashed through the water in the driveway. Men yanked the lines out of the back hall. I looked past them, up at the fire spitting out of the eaves. The roof shingles melted and bubbled.

I laughed out loud. For a few minutes, I actually hadn't thought about money owed or deals not done.

I felt like someone was watching me. I looked up to the second story dining room window, the same place I'd made my futile attempt to save George. Fire now engulfed the entire second floor.

At least fire was consistent. Unlike the rest of my life.

I kept staring and a calmness came over me. The window was full of fire, but in the middle it was different. It held a greenish hue. More than that, the green held its shape. It was a vibration, a wave, then it rounded and I swear I saw a head and shoulders and two arms and hands resting on the window sill. It had no face, but I was sure it looked down at me.

I rose to my feet. Here I was between the disaster that was my life and the tragedy that was the failed rescue of little George, and this thing brought me peace. I didn't care if it was an angel or death itself. I had to find out more.

I shrugged off my harness and grabbed an abandoned one from the ground. The gauge said one quarter full. I flipped it on my back and slipped my arms through the straps. On the run I secured my mask, turned the valve, and ran up the stairs. The voices that called for me were devoured by the sounds of the fire: the roar snapping like a thousand hungry mouths, chomping, chewing, and digesting the house. I hurried up the stairs, yanked on the railings, and made it to the second-floor landing. I looked into the kitchen and there was no smoke this time. A lake of orange and red whirled over the ceiling. I fell to my belly and did a frog crawl. I felt like I was in boiling water. The fire overhead roared. I was inching toward my death, but I didn't care. The green flame had called me and hinted at something I had to have.

I made it to the doorway between the kitchen and dining room. Behind me I heard the lathes that held up the ceiling start to snap. Plaster and lathe fell with a boom. The water on the floor heaved up and slopped over my back and down my neck. It scalded me and I cried out in the silence of my face piece.

Debris barred my exit. My bell rang. I realized there was no retreat and my strength drained from my body. I rolled over on my back. At least my tank kept me out of hot water. Fire loomed above me, such a beautiful thing, full of energy, full of life and death. Maybe it contained the peace I sought.

Again everything was cool and peaceful. There was flame over me, all around me, but it was green as burning phosphorus. No, more like a river of liquid emeralds, cool and soothing, and distorting the light, teasing me, coyly withholding its secrets. My problems softened and dripped away and for the first time in a very long time, I was happy.

I closed my eyes and knew that all was well.

CHAPTER THREE

Fresh air hit my face and I started hacking so hard I thought I'd spit out my lungs. My feet dragged across the concrete. To my right, Willie crouched under my armpit with my arm draped over his shoulder. His gloved hand was clamped down tight on my wrist. Under his helmet, rivulets of water dribbled off his midnight face.

Another firefighter ran up and took my other arm and brought me to the rear running board of Engine 17. I bent over and retched my dinner onto my boots. Willie's hands were all over me, pulling off my helmet, helping me shed my tank, unclasping my fire coat. Someone jammed a mouthpiece on me. I leaned back against the rig and sucked in cool oxygen.

Willie stood with one hand on my shoulder and one hand on the rig. The adrenaline-fueled energy drained out of him and once more he looked old and tired. "If you ever do that again," he paused to take a breath, "I'm going to kill you."

"How …?"

"Willie heard you were in trouble," the other firefighter said. "We couldn't have stopped him if we wanted to."

My eyes misted over. "For a skinny black spasm, you are one crazy motherfucker."

"Fuck you, too, Sam," he said, then leaned over, grabbed my neck, and kissed the top of my head.

***

I sat at the firehouse kitchen table with my hand around a mug of coffee. Big Daddy sat across from me, a mountain of serious. Willie went over to the cupboard and pulled out a bottle. He leaned over my shoulder and dribbled amber liquid into my mug.

"It'll put some hair on your chest," Willie said. He tipped the bottle into own his mug and Rich's. "You didn't see nothing, right, L.T?"

Al raised his head from his desk, a distracted look on his face. "What was that, Willie?"

"See what I mean?" Willie said. He plopped into the chair beside me and placed the bottle on the floor by his feet.

"I was hooking up at the hydrant so I couldn't see it," Rich said, "but the guys said you made one hell of a rescue, Sam."

But I didn't save George.

"Hell of a rescue," Willie said, clinking his mug against mine. "Now you want to tell me why the fuck you ran back inside?"

Thinking back on it, it didn't make any sense. "I thought I saw something."

Rich shook his head. "This ain't right. Next time, Willie, you stay with Sam and Al. I can hook up to the hydrant by myself."

"We got to change what we're doing," Willie said, nodding at Al. He was right. Al had ditched me. It was stuff like that that was going to get one of us killed.

The phone rang. Al answered it. He listened, then put it down. "Sam, that was the chief. He wants me to check with you."

"About what?"

"Do you want to go to the hospital? Chief says you can take a couple days off if you need it."

If I went off on an injury, I'd be stuck on home confinement. I had too much to do. "I'm good," I said.

"Chief wants me to write the report. Says you might get a commendation."

I went from numb to full boil in a second. I stood up and walked over to the desk. "You're gonna write me up, Al?"

"Sure, Sam. Maybe you'll get an award."

"How will you know what to write?"

"I don't know. Just what happened, that's all."

"But you didn't actually see anything, did you, Al?"

"I guess. But I can just take what everybody is saying—"

"You left me, Al."

"I told you. My tank malfunctioned. Sometimes water gets inside the valve."

"You couldn't say something? Tap me on the shoulder? You couldn't yell out, hey, Sam, I'm fucking ditching you in the middle of the fire?"

He looked up at me, his face frozen in a weak smile. His skin flushed red from his chin to the back of his scalp. "I figured, you know, with Captain Sikes and his crew ...."

I grabbed the front of his shirt, yanked him out of the chair, and bent him over the desk. "You want to tell me what the fuck you're good for?"

Hands clutched my shoulders. I felt a vise around my waist. Rich yanked me off my feet and swung me around.

"You are a useless piece of shit, you know that?" I spit out. I struggled against Rich, but it was like wrestling with a bear.

Willie darted in front of me, putting his hands on my chest. "Listen

24

guys, it's been one hell of a night. We might not be thinking straight."

"I'm thinking just fine," I said.

Willie's voice boomed through the kitchen. "I fucking said you're not." He wagged a finger under my nose. "Now you go upstairs and chill and let the L.T. do his work."

"Come on, Sam," Rich said. With his arm over my shoulder he led me out of the kitchen.

***

After a shower, I told the guys I'd stand watch until morning. Since my mind was racing a thousand miles per hour, I didn't think I could sleep anyways. I sat in the recliner, chewing over my problems, while some lady on a cooking show prattled on about how to chop garlic.

Fucking Al. If he was gonna be a chickenshit, he should get his ass out of the 'hood. Maybe if he'd have brought the line into the dining room and given me some cover, I might've gotten to George a minute earlier. Maybe the little boy would have had a chance.

What had happened to me at the fire? I might have imagined green flame and flashes, but not how I felt, not the peace it brought me.

My mind must have been twisted from all the stress in my life. Losing George, that just pushed me over the edge.

I wanted to call Cindy to check on Rae, but there was no sense waking them up. I was already on Cindy's shit list.

Anyways I didn't have time for this. Come eight a.m., I had to straighten out some real problems.

Rain tapped against the windows. Rain is good luck for firefighters. People stay inside and save the crazy stuff for another day.

***

I woke up at six thirty with a start. My head felt like mush. Time to make the coffee for the day crew and get ready for another wonderful morning. I pushed myself out of the chair, slipped into my shoes, and made my way to the coffee pot by the sink.

A few minutes later, the pot gurgled and that wonderful wake up coffee odor filled the kitchen. I stood over the sink, cleaning up some leftover dishes. The rain had turned into a downpour. It made jabbing sounds on the pavement in the parking lot.

I heard something else. Several weak taps coming from the back door.

Could be just someone from the day shift who'd forgotten his key. The captain sometimes got in early. I walked out the kitchen door and through the narrow locker room that led to the rear entrance.

I swung the door open and froze. Before me stood a girl, head down, rain slapping against her scalp. Her golden hair laid flat against her head. She looked up at me like she'd come to apologize.

Oh, my God. It was Farrah Fawcett.

No, that was another one of my delusions. She stood up to my chin, which would have made her just under six foot. Farrah barely broke five-seven. Her skin had a lemon shade and was almost translucent. And she was longer limbed.

Her green eyes flashed at me. "I need your help, Sam Carver," she said, then collapsed into my arms. I scooped her up and held her like a baby.

It wasn't unusual for drug addicts, drunks, and other lost people to come to beg at the firehouse door. Usually I sent them away or called an ambulance. But this lady, well, she was different.

She wore a fire coat about ten sizes too big. It fell to the sides as I cradled her. Under the coat, she was buck naked. Her body was as sensuous as a panther's.

What the fuck?

Smudges marked her skin. Sometimes prostitutes ran away from their pimps, sometimes they were beaten up. But even if they were young, they were worn down people and their bodies showed it.

This lady was startlingly beautiful.

I took her into the kitchen, set her on her bare feet, and guided her into a chair. She looked around the room and smacked her lips, the same way I had seen people who came out of anesthetic do. When I was sure she wouldn't tip over, I brought her a cup of coffee and a bowl of leftover cobbler.

"Good," she said after she sipped the coffee. She dabbed two fingers into the cobbler and licked them. "Very good."

I looked up at the clock. Quarter to seven. In a few minutes, the day shift would be coming in. The last thing I needed was for the captain to catch me with a naked woman in the firehouse. I leaned over and snapped shut the clasps on the soggy coat.

"Miss, is there someone I can call for you? Are you hurt?"

She shook her head, grabbed the bowl, held it under her chin, and used her hands to scoop the cobbler into her mouth.

"Where did you get the coat?"

She looked up at me with innocent eyes. Peach syrup surrounded her lips. "I found it."

I sniffed. "You smell of fire." It wasn't just from the coat. Those smudges on her face and legs were soot.

She kept her eyes on me as she chewed.

"What happened to your clothes?"

She nodded. "You're right. I'm going to need clothes."

I knelt down so that we were face to face. "Miss?"

"Alana."

"Alana, you can't stay here. Tell me what you need. I want to help you."

She studied me so solemnly that I almost didn't notice the syrup dripping down her chin.

"I know you do, Sam," she said. She moved quickly, smoothly, naturally, leaning forward, wrapping her arms around my shoulders and kissing me. For a moment everything was perfect and I didn't see the soot on her cheek. The cobbler mingled with the wonderful taste of her mouth and I had an angel in my arms.

I had no time for fantasy. I pushed her away and stood up quickly. "How do you know my name?"

"You were very brave at the fire."

I hadn't even checked the news. By now everybody probably knew about it.

Was she some kind of stalker?

"Listen, I can call a women's shelter. But it's almost seven and you've got to go."

"Please don't."

"Don't what?"

"Don't send me away."

"Are you in trouble?"

"Lots of trouble."

I stepped toward the desk and picked up the phone. "I'm sorry, Miss. I'll call the Red Cross. They'll help you." I heard someone open the front door. The German drinking tune that Captain Rolf sang every morning rumbled through the apparatus floor.

The rear door slammed. I looked up and all that was left of her was a half empty cup of coffee, a bowl licked clean, and a puddle under the chair she'd sat in.

Captain Rolf stepped into the kitchen and stopped abruptly, his stomach protruding, his heavy jowls shaking.

"Coffee's down, Captain," I said.

He humphed and surveyed the room. He was a suspicious motherfucker. Swayback, he strolled over to the sink and noticed the puddle under the chair. "Did you fucking piss on the floor or something? Make sure you clean up your dishes. My crew sure as hell isn't gonna pick up your mess."

***

Rain thumped against my windshield. Fatigue crept up my legs and coursed through my body. From the car radio, a female disc jockey plied her husky voice to announce the next Lionel Richie song.

I considered my life. I was like a sucker walking down the midway of some crazy carnival. Taking chances, crapping out, playing again with other people's money.

I'd catch an hour of sleep at home, then I'd call Janice. She had the hots for me. She was ten years older but had just broken up with her man—and I knew she had money. If I banged her real good, maybe she'd cough up a grand. That would keep the Italians off my ass for a while. I also had to call the developers and keep everything cool with them. Maybe I should stop by my dad's to see if he had spoken to Uncle Bill yet.

And Rae. I had to see Rae. Maybe if I brought Cindy a couple hundred, she'd cool down. I needed to see my baby.

The colors I saw at the fire, the crazy lady at the firehouse, that was just my mind fucking with me because of all the pressure I was under.

I pulled in front of my apartment. The engine stuttered when I turned it off. I kept the radio on and just leaned my head back against the seat.

With me, it was always something. Would I ever find some peace?

The Temptations came on the radio, "Just My Imagination." I sang along.

"I like that," I heard from the back seat and almost jumped through the roof.

I whirled around. "Alana." Even though she was probably a stalker, she made me smile.

"That song. Very pretty. You know, once you started driving, it got really comfy back here." She rested her chin on the top of the front seat.

"The Crown Vics have good heaters," I said. "You want to tell me what the fuck you're doing?" She was one fine woman, but I didn't have time for this.

"Is this where you live?" She bent her head down and looked through the side window at the row of two-story brick apartments.

"Yes—I mean, no. You didn't answer my question."

"I want to see it." She pushed open her door and swung her legs out, then looked back to me. "Would you mind giving me a hand? My legs are still a little wobbly."

I'd had enough. I threw my door open, slammed it hard, and stormed over to the other side of the car. Her bare legs dangled over the edge and she dabbed her toes into a puddle of water. Taking her wrists,

I yanked her to her feet.

"Oh," she said. "You're strong. I like that." She swayed and steadied herself with her hands on my shoulders.

She looked up at me and opened her wide mouth into a beautiful smile. She blinked when the rain fell into her eyes.

"You don't understand. I got enough going on," I said. The cool rain brought a fresh smell to the air.

She looked straight up, stuck out her tongue and giggled. "It tickles."

"If I take on one more thing, I feel like I'm going to break."

She started unsnapping the clasps on her coat.

"What are you doing?"

"I bet it will feel good on my skin," she said.

I took her wrists and gave her a shake. "You are not coming inside."

"Yes, I am."

"Are you crazy?"

"I don't think so. I know you're not going to leave me out in the rain. Not when I need you so much."

***

I leaned against the bathroom door in my apartment, shaking my head. It was almost nine and I had a shit load of stuff to do.

I heard a sweet voice humming and water splashing.

I set my mouth inches from the door and spoke forcefully. "Are you all right, Alana?"

"Oh, yes. This is just yummy." She laughed and splashed again.

"That's great. 'Cause I got to get you out of here right away."

She screamed a childish, painful scream.

"Alana, what's wrong?"

"It hurts so much," she said.

I shouldered the door open, expecting to see blood. She sat in the tub, her feet kicking the water, waving her hands to the side, her head from neck to nose covered in shampoo.

"What's wrong?"

"My eyes. It burns so much."

"Come on, Alana."

"Please."

What kind of game was she playing? I knelt down and grabbed a pitcher that I kept beside the tub and scooped out some bath water. "Lean forward."

"Hurry!"

She hunched her shoulders and curved her long neck. The ends of her golden hair fell into the bubbles. I poured water over her head.

"It still hurts. A lot."

"You're supposed to keep your eyes closed."

"I didn't know."

Was she stupid or something? Or was this a trick to get me to wash her? Maybe get me in bed then steal my money?

It wasn't going to work. For one thing, I didn't have any money.

I'd play along but keep an eye on her. Which wasn't hard to do, seeing she was as gorgeous as Farrah on her best day. And naked and soaking wet.

"It's okay now," I said.

She raised her face, all pure and slick, while keeping her eyes squinched shut. "You sure?" she said, then blinked and smiled. "I guess you're always saving people."

"Alana, don't you use shampoo?"

"Should I?"

"You're supposed to close your eyes."

"But it smelled so good."

I picked up the bottle and sniffed. "Honeysuckle."

"See? It's not my fault."

I stood up. "You think you can get out of the tub without any more drama? I left some clothes for you on the toilet. You put them on, then you got to go."

She looked down and nodded sadly. "Okay, Sam."

***

I sat on the kitchen chair. Her song lulled me like a breeze in the forest. I felt like I was going to nod off and my face was going to slam against the table. The door creaked open and she walked into the room with a big grin on her face. She pushed up on her toes and twirled. The red dress I left for her just barely covered her bottom and clung to her skin because she was soaking wet.

"Didn't you dry yourself?"

"Was I supposed to?"

Growling, I jumped up, stomped into the bathroom, snatched a few towels, and went back to my chair in the kitchen.

"Come here," I said, pointing to the floor in front of me. I meant it to sound impatient.

She complied. I rubbed down her bare legs. She giggled when I dried the soles of her feet. I commanded her to bend over and I passed the towel through her hair. Next, I held her hands and dried her arms. She had long graceful fingers.

"Now what?" She asked, rolling from heel to toe, swinging her arms back and forth.

I grabbed her hand and led her into the living room and over to the couch. I pushed on her lightly and she plopped down. After I set one towel over her shoulders and one on her lap, I sat down next to her.

"Comfy," she said. "But a little cold."

"Because you're wet. Once you dry off, you've got to go. Now don't move," I told her. I leaned over her and ran a brush through her hair.

"Ow!"

I stopped and dangled the brush in front of her face. "You want to do it?"

She shook her head. I started again. She yelped. Maybe I was working my frustrations out on her. I went slower, remembering when I used to do Rae's hair. When I came to a tangle, I lightened up. After a few minutes, I set the brush down on the coffee table. "That's the best I can do," I said.

"How do I look?"

I made a simple part in the middle of her head and tried to draw her long hair down equally on both sides. Her eyes shone, her unblemished skin blushed pink, her mouth pouted thoughtfully, and her button nose was positioned perfectly in the middle.

"You look incredible," I said. "But it's time to go."

"I don't have anywhere to go."

"No family? No friends? Nobody you work with?"

"Just you."

I leaned back. "You're talking crazy. And I have too much to do."

"I know that you have a lot on your mind."

I turned to her and stared. "Now, it's stuff like that that makes me really think you're not well."

"But I know all about you, Sam."

I didn't think she was hiding a pair of scissors behind her back, but she was showing definite crazy stalker tendencies.

"You want to tell me about it?" She reached out and brushed the back of her hand over my cheek.

"Alana, you're starting to freak me out here."

"Why did you try to save him?"

That went right through me.

"It's not the time ...." But it was. I fought it but I ached to tell somebody.

"All the others, they didn't want to try. But you did."

"It's what we're supposed to do," I said quietly. "Listen, Alana, I really have a lot to do."

"Do you know why I chose you?"

"I don't know what you're talking about."

"You would have traded your life for his."

I looked down and tapped the brush against my knee. "Maybe his life would have worked out better than mine." My eyes misted over. That happens sometimes after a fire, with all the smoke.

Fatigue flooded through me. Dreams crept up. I saw George running through a playground, his Star Wars T-shirt two sizes too big. He found secure footing with his sneaker on the monkey bars, climbing hand over hand, watching each step. He kept on up in a zig zag, until he was near the top, where my little Rae reached down to grab his hand.

Alana slipped next to me, her lips whispering a slow sweet song, her hands sliding over my face, through my hair and down my neck.

"Alana, this isn't a good idea."

Her fingers and lips were a blur of wonderful comfort. "Shh. I'm going to take good care of you."

***

It just kind of happened. She took my hand and we drifted to the bedroom. It was like I was hovering on the ceiling, watching myself, as I pulled back the sheets and shed my clothes. She sloughed off her dress and there she stood in all her glory. The skin on her legs was as smooth as the skin on her stomach and as unblemished as the skin on the back of her hands. She was mostly legs and arms. When she moved, her sleek body swayed like the limbs of a tree in a spring breeze. Before I knew it, I was on my back and she straddled me, rocking, keeping her green eyes locked on mine. She took in each breath like she was sniffing expensive cognac. Her head tilted left and right as if she delighted in every sound, delighted even in the drafts of my bedroom. We made slow, wonderful, hypnotic love.

When it was over, she fell down next to me. Her perspiration looked like glitter. I ran my hand over her cheek.

"Who are you?"

"I'm Alana."

"I've got to know."

"Let's play a game. I let you ask me one thing and I tell you. Then I get to ask you."

"I don't play games."

"Do it for me."

"Okay. But you have to tell me the truth."

"I won't ever lie to you, Sam."

"Why did you follow me?"

"I saw this man do this wonderful thing and I wanted to be close to

32

him."

"But what about—"

She pressed her finger to my lips and said, "Only one question at a time. My turn."

"Go on."

"Tell me all of it," she said.

My stomach jumped. "What are you talking about?"

"What did you think about when I asked that?"

"Nothing. It's a weird question."

"You promised not to lie." She bopped my nose with her finger.

"Alana ...." It felt like the heat had been sucked out of the bedroom. I shivered.

She moved in close, threw her arm around my shoulder. "I understand. You've never told it before."

"Please ...."

"I won't be mad. I won't judge."

"It all so confusing."

"Trust me."

I blurted out about my trouble sleeping. When I thought I was done, she just nodded, and I blurted out some more. Why couldn't I sleep? What haunted me?

Soon I was rattling on and I couldn't stop. I told her about my dad, how he forced religion on me, how I felt like I had to rebel. When I paused and looked up, she simply nodded and whispered, "Go on."

I told her about Cindy and how much that hurt. I told her about the accident, the rehab, the drugs. I couldn't stop. I told her about how shitty I'd been to a whole bunch of women, some of them hoes but some really nice ladies. I told her about the money I owed, the drugs I took, the married women I'd laid with, the plans for my dad's property, how it wasn't really stealing but just taking advantage of our assets.

I finally ran out of steam. My breath came in loud hums. Sweat dripped off my lip.

"You must think I'm a monster," I said.

"I don't think that at all. But I want you to finish."

"No more, please."

"Tell me about George."

I laughed. That was easy. "I just wanted to help."

"Why?"

"I don't know. Sometimes you get a medal."

"The truth," she said.

I took a deep breath. "He needed me."

"What else?"

"It's nothing."

"Look again."

I hadn't thought of it for years, but it was right before me now.

"I'd rather not."

"Are you afraid, Sam Carver?"

The words flowed out of me; I had no control over them. "When I was little, I would see my dad do all these good things. He did marriages, was with the young when they came into the world and helped send people off when they left. He always knew the right words to say. People would shake his hand and slap him on the back. They'd treat me different than the other kids because I was his son.

"One day I was sneaking around the rectory, hiding in this closet, where he kept the old Christmas ornaments. I heard something and peaked out the door. There was my father, talking away. But he didn't use his big preacher voice. He was whispering. And a lady was with him. I still remember her name. Mrs. Alderson. I thought she was ancient, but she might have been thirty-five. Her husband ran a dry cleaner's down the street. They whispered and laughed. My dad talked real low and soothing, almost like he did to me when I was sick. But ...."

I wiped the sweat from my brow.

"It's okay, Sam," Alana said.

"But he bent her over one of the extra pews he kept in the rectory. And the two of them kept laughing and whispering. Then he dropped his pants. He was standing there with Mrs. Alderson's butt in the air and his pants around his ankles and he was still wearing his sports jacket."

"Go on, Sam."

"I don't know. It was like there was an earthquake in my little boy world. It was all lies, the big-voiced sermons, the pats on the back, saying grace over supper, even when he kissed my mother on the cheek.

"I must have made some noise because the next thing I know he's yanking up his pants and charging over and swatting my behind and calling me a little sneak. And if he ever catches me sneaking again, or if he ever hears me repeat one word of this, he's going to take his belt and, so help him God, rip every bit of skin off my back and rub salt into it. But what frightened me the most was the look on his face. His lips were twisted. His teeth looked gray and rotting and poisonous. I jumped out and ran for the door. I felt the toe of his shoe strike my tailbone."

"Then what?"

"I ran home and cried. I cried and cried. Then I stopped crying. And from then on when I heard him preach, I heard my father, but I heard a little bit of the devil. And if Jesus's church was tainted then everything was tainted. Everything in this whole fucking world."

"Except George?"

I looked up at her. "Maybe God doesn't care about the rest of us. But I wish he would leave the kids alone."

CHAPTER FOUR

Talk about craziness. I slept hard until I heard her singing a light, heavenly song. I looked up, fought to focus, and saw a hazy image of an angel. I rubbed my eyes and there was Alana standing at the front window, tapping at the glass. She was naked.

"What are you doing?"

She stopped and turned to me, looking surprised. "I think I saw a spider."

I rushed over and pulled down the shade. "You can't show the whole neighborhood all your stuff," I said.

"I don't have any stuff except the dress you gave me."

"Your hooters. Your butt. We'll have every guy on the street pounding on the door trying to get a piece."

She poked her nose in the air and sounded slighted. "I do not give out pieces. It's all of Alana or nothing at all."

I looked at the clock. "Shit, Alana, it's four in the afternoon." I grabbed my pants and slid into them.

"Did I do something to make you angry?"

"No. You're wonderful. I'm just late, that's all. But put your clothes on. And stay away from the windows."

Sure, she was wonderful. Inconvenient, too. If I didn't straighten some stuff out, I was in deep shit.

First, I called my chief and asked him if I could take the night off. I told him I was exhausted from the fire, which was mostly true. Next, I called my date for that night, Janice, with the intention of telling her I'd be right over. But after my afternoon with Alana, I just couldn't do it. It's not that I didn't think I could perform. Hell, no. But something about it didn't seem right. Using the fire as an excuse, I told her I'd call her back after I got some sleep.

I threw on my shirt, grabbed my keys, and walked to the front door. Alana came out of the bedroom with a puppy dog look on her face.

"I got to take care of some stuff," I said. "You sure you don't have any place to go?"

"No."

I didn't have time to argue. "Look. You can stay here until I get back. Keep away from the windows and don't answer the door. And please put some clothes on. I'll bring back something to eat. Think about where you're going to stay."

As I drove down the beaten streets of the east side of Buffalo, I realized something. I didn't feel too bad. Usually, the recovery from a working fire in the middle of the night was a little like a hangover: it took a day or two to get it out of your system. And the thing that happened with George, I'd never forget. But in spite of that, I felt like I'd slept through the weekend.

Once I'd made love to this girl from Jamaica who was into some crazy voodoo hoodoo that they use down there. Her skin shone deep blue-black, her butt hung high, and her muscles rippled like those of a cheetah. While we did it, she played a record of this chanting music and she burned candles with sweet, twisted odors. After the sex, I fell into a kind of stupor and slept deep. Maybe Alana did some cult-ish thing, drugged me or used hypnotism. Whatever. Just because Alana and I shared one wild afternoon, I wasn't going to get carried away.

I parked in front of Lucy's Place, a one-story shack of a restaurant on a side road next to the railroad tracks. The steps slanted to one side so I held on to the two-by-four railing for dear life. I knocked on the kitchen door and walked in. A rancid odor assaulted my nose, and I knew Lucy had been cleaning chitlins. On one wall, a metal table separated a refrigerator from a sink and a stove. The deep frier spit bubbles of grease. Lucy obscured the stove, all hips and bouncing arm fat. Her pudgy fingers worked a butcher's knife on a pile of chicken. She turned to me with her full moon face. "Where you've been, sweet pea?"

"Kind of busy." I pecked her on the cheek, reached over her drooping bosom to the fried chicken. She swatted my hand with the dull side of the knife.

"I thought you and me were tight," I said. My hand stung like hell.

"Aw, you know you're my sweet pea, but you better leave my chicken alone or I'll cut you. This is for customers tonight and if I run out, I can't pay the bills."

"How about a little taste?" I came in close and put my hands on her shoulders.

"Can't you see I'm working here? Why didn't you come over the house this weekend when I was expecting you?"

"I got real busy."

"Busy with who?"

"Just business, baby. You know I can't get enough of your sweet stuff." I reached down and squeezed a handful of ass. She had plenty left over.

She pushed me on my shoulders. "Go on, git," she said. I looked at her sadly. "See that chicken on the counter?" she said. "Take that. I burned it a little."

"Oh, so I'm your sweet pea, but I get the burned stuff?"

"Ain't nothing wrong with it, just a little too crispy. Now get out of here and let me do my work." She slammed the business end of the knife on the cutting board. "And you better come by this weekend. Don't make me come looking for you."

"I love you too, Lucy," I said. I dropped the chicken in a bag and stopped at the door next to a stack of pie boxes. I grabbed one, put it under my arm and ran.

"You are going to hell for sure, Sam Carver." She yelled like a train whistle.

"So I've been told," I said, to myself since I was out the door.

Without some money, the Italians would be breathing down my neck. Or breaking it. So next stop was a check cashing place that ran numbers on the side and loaned a little money from a converted gas station. Inside on the right wall, there was a counter that was screened off. Under a lamp in the middle of the room six old men leaned over a small table, turning cards, throwing out money and curses.

I walked over to the rear door that was guarded by a mountain with a shaved head and a Raiders jacket. "Buddy, how's it hanging?" I asked. "You think I could stick my head in and say hey to Mona?" It was best to be polite to Buddy since he stood six-five and weighed about four-fifty.

Buddy stared at me for a minute before he opened the door a crack and peered in. "Someone wants to see you."

Mona's melodic voice wafted out of the back room like a jackhammer on steel plate. "Tell them I'm fucking busy."

Buddy spoke to me like I didn't matter. "You got to get the fuck out."

I stretched over his shoulder and shouted., "It's me, Mona, Sam Carver."

Mona cackled and called for me to come in. I squeezed past Buddy's sloppy gut. Mona sat in the middle of a long table. Her boney hands flipped through a stack of greenbacks.

Mona might have been sixty but looked ten years older. She was reed thin and wore a red wig. Her skin drooped on her face and her yellow teeth clamped down on a cigar.

"Hey, baby doll. You okay? I saw the news. Everybody is so proud of you. It's good to see a brother get some credit in this town."

"It was a rough night," I said.

"Thank the Lord you're fine. I prayed for that little boy."

"Thank you."

"I hate to rush you, baby doll, but this is kind of a busy time here. What can I do you for?"

"My credit still good?"

She took the cigar out of her mouth and laughed through a throat full of phlegm. "Come on, baby doll. You know Mona ain't no fool."

"I don't need much. A taste until I get this deal done."

"A taste?" She jabbed the cigar at me. "I like you, Sam. And your mom was a sweet lady. Your father, on the other hand, had more than a bit of the devil in him. Seems to go hand in hand with preachers."

"Dad's in a bad way."

"And I feel real sorry for him." She took a puff and let it drift over her face. "But I got to tell it like it is, Sam. You couldn't borrow a quarter for a pay toilet. I hear things, you know."

"Mona, that's just street gossip."

"Whatever you say, baby doll. I know a lot that goes on in this town, you know what I mean? I know you owe the Italians big and they ain't happy."

"Please, Mona. You got to give me something. I got a steady job."

"I'll give you something. A little advice. You better straighten things around quick, Sam, or the whole house is gonna come tumbling on top of you. Now, Buddy here," she said, summoning him with a motion of her hand, "is gonna show you the way out. You take care of yourself, hear?"

So I scored a free dinner but didn't get the money. That was fifty-fifty.

At Dad's house, I let him prattle on. "You know, son, your mother was never a woman to take a likening to cats. But I have to revisit the issue because last night, right out of our garage, I saw a rat as big as a taxi. Rats will run just on the scent of a cat, but if I were this rat, I wouldn't run for nothing. Looked more like a raccoon than a cat."

"Maybe it was a raccoon," I said, looking at my watch.

"Now that's just dern ridiculous. You need woods for raccoons, and there ain't no woods around here. Now, time and again, they might come down the railroad tracks. But I promise you if I see a 'coon here I'm gonna take out my three fifty-seven and blow a hole through his hide, just like I was gonna do last night to that rat, except I seemed to have misplaced my firearm."

"You lost your pistol?"

"For a minute. Someone put it in the linen drawer in the dining room. I ain't never kept it there."

"Dad, if you discharge your firearm in your backyard, they *are* going to lock you up." *And send you to a home where they will take everything you have and I'll never get to sell the church property.*

"I don't go for things not being in their right places. Which is why I said, if you recall, that I didn't want no stranger traipsing around in the house that your mother took so much care to furnish. Now, there's a man a few doors down. He's a widower like me. He has this woman come in once a month. If I could just find the number." He started fumbling through the papers on the end table next to his chair.

Maybe I should have asked to borrow his gun and shoot myself right there.

"Dad." My voice was firm.

He turned to me, his eyes fixed on mine. "Don't take that tone with your father. I can still whip your ass."

"Did you talk to Uncle Billy?"

"Who?"

"Your brother."

"Billy? Oh sure, I talked to him. Funny thing is, he and I are in the same boat. You and me got to take a ride to see him. You'd do that for your dad, wouldn't you? Not many chances left. Now if you'll excuse me, it's almost eight, and I better get my sleep now because I can't rightly sleep past five a.m." He put his palm on the arm rest and tried to push himself up.

"Dad, it's important. Give me a minute, okay?"

He settled back in, folded his hands in his lap patiently. "Why sure son. I always got time for my boy."

"What did Uncle Billy say about giving me power of attorney?"

"Well, he said a lot of things. There's the issue of fiduciary control and drawing out the exact duties of the responsible parties. There was the issue of your Aunt Sadie. You remember her, don't you? Used to send us all those God-awful scarves at Christmas. We had a closet full of ugly scarves and your mother, God rest her soul, wouldn't let me throw them in the fire."

I steered the conversation away from Aunt Sadie's scarves and back to the matter at hand, telling him how making me power of attorney would just improve his chances of staying in his home the rest of his life, how I could act more quickly in an emergency, how I was the one child of his who stayed in Buffalo to watch over him. I'd gone on for about twenty minutes when I heard him snore.

Dad's head leaned against the back cushion of the couch. His eyes were shut, his mouth hung open. I looked at the clock. Eight-twenty. If I woke him now, he'd never get up by five to do whatever old man things he had scheduled in the morning. I walked over to him, slipped my arms under him, and, careful to lift with my legs, carried him through the dining room. He barely weighed one-twenty. He felt like a sack of bones. Turning sideways down the hall, I managed to make it to his room without cracking his head against the door frame. I set him down, removed his shoes, and pulled the blanket up to his neck. I looked down at him with love and hate and pity. "You owe me this, Dad," I said quietly. I turned to leave and reached to flip off the switch by the door. Hanging on the wall was an old black and white photo of Mom and Dad. His hair was slicked back. Her bangs swung over her head from one of those toxic treatments Black women used to use. On the other side was a color print, miniature me in the middle and my two sisters. We wore matching Christmas sweaters and elf hats.

I flipped out the light and walked out.

***

I stopped by the firehouse on the way home. I parked on the apron and stuck my head out the window. Rich and Willie sat on the bench out front.

"What's up?" I said.

Rich looked past me. He held a camera rangefinder up to his eye.

"What the fuck is he doing?" I asked Willie.

"Let Peeping Tom here tell you," Willie said.

"This is like a mini telescope. That girl across the street showers about now, right before she goes out."

"I can't believe this," I said.

"You ever seen her tits? The girl is a force of nature."

"You wouldn't be such a pervert if you got some at home," I said.

"My wife's having her period. I think it started at Easter," Rich said.

"Did I miss anything?" I asked.

"Where do you want me to start?" Willie said. "Right after shift change, we got a call down on Gibson Street. You know where those gang bangers hang out?"

Rich arched his back and stretched his tree trunk arms over his head. "Wannabes. None of them have ever been in a real fight."

"So there's about a dozen of them," Willie said, "shouting and threatening and your momma this and motherfucker that. So we pull up next to them, all lights and siren, and they fall back to the sidewalk. Now, you know your by-the-book Lieutenant, he wants to call the cops and have them start shooting. So I say, Al, give me a minute to talk some sense into them."

"Willie set them straight," Rich said.

"I go up to this one kid who looked like he was in charge, but, hell, they all looked wet behind the ears. So I say, listen son, if you don't move, the police are coming and you'll end up in jail and they might crack some heads in the process."

"You're not going to believe what the kid said," Rich said.

"What did he say?" I asked.

Willie shook his head. "He said, 'Why don't you go away, old man?' Sam, I almost lost my mind."

"I thought it was gonna be a homicide," Rich said.

"I guess I *did* lose it," Willie said. "I called his momma a hoe and said he should try and find his pa if the son of a bitch was still around because I was fixin' to whup ass on his entire family."

"Good thing you kept things calm," I said.

"I grabbed the axe off the rig," Rich said. "I thought it was gonna be a brawl."

"Wouldn't be no brawl," Willie said. "Back in the day, Big Daddy and me would have cleared that whole street out without breaking a sweat."

Rich said, "So one of the kids comes over and he says to Willie, 'I know you, Mr. Goodman. My dad talks about you.' And he's all, 'Let's make friends now.' The kids back off the street and I'm holding on to Willie's coat 'cause he's rearing up to run the Kentucky Derby."

"You're too old to fight, Willie," I said.

"Sometimes you gotta do what you gotta do," Willie said.

"That's just the start," Rich said.

"Yeah, from there it got really fun," Willie said. "We got a call that somebody saw two naked white guys stumbling into somebody's yard."

"Two naked white guys?" I said. "This isn't one of Rich's sexual fantasies?"

"Two skinny white guys bare ass stumbling through people's yards," Willie said. "I thought Mr. Simon's pit bull was gonna tear their nuts off."

"So how did they get away?"

"Hey, they pay me to put out fires," Willie said, "not to mud wrestle Dumb and Dumber."

"Did the police get them," I asked.

"As you can imagine, they rushed over about forty-five minutes too late," Willie said. "Guess stumbling naked white guys aren't a high priority."

"Let one brother take his shirt off in the middle of the white folks," Rich said, "and they'll send the SWAT team."

"Well said, Malcolm X," I told him.

"Tell him the other stuff," Rich said, still scanning the second-floor apartment across the street.

"You know the green flame the L.T. was talking about?"

"Yeah? They figure out what it was?"

"No, but maybe they will now," Willie said. "'Cause there were two more of them tonight. Ran right through the plaza."

"It's probably not anything too toxic," Rich said. "And what the hell, the only people who live around here are Black, so there's nothing to worry about."

"So I didn't miss much," I said.

"Oh, you missed more than that," Rich said. "Some of your friends drove by."

"How do you know they were my friends?"

"They drove a black El Dorado," Rich said. "They wore black suits and sunglasses. And neither Willie or me owe money to the mob."

Willie shook his head. "You better take care of business, cousin."

"Well, that's good news," I said and started to pull away.

"Don't you want to hear the rest of it?" Rich said.

"Probably not," I said.

"Cindy and Rae stopped by to see you."

I drove away. Thank God I had taken the night off.

I really did want to see Rae. But I was in no mood to rehash the you-owe-me-money discussion.

***

I drove home and pulled down my block. The streetlights snapped on. The smell of ribs snuck up on me. Barbeque Bob, as tall as me but sloppy fat, wore a white apron and chef's hat as he worked his grill in the front of his driveway.

I had made no progress. I really wanted to just relax with Alana, but maybe I should call Janice and tap that hole. Maybe if I softened her up, she'd spring for a loan.

Deep in my own thoughts, I didn't notice the blue Toyota parked two doors down. I pulled into the driveway. The Crown Vic coughed when I turned off the key.

Chicken and pie in hand, I climbed up the steps and tried the door. It was open. My heart jumped. I felt it from head to toe: trouble was coming.

I swung open the door and saw all the trouble I could handle, because past the living room and through the archway, Alana sat at the kitchen table.

Cindy sat across from her.

My first thought was to make a run for it. But Rae scampered through the house and latched on to my leg. "Oh, Daddy, Mommy and I were so worried about you. You were so brave. Everybody's talking about it. You're the best daddy in the world." She grabbed my elbow and tugged me toward the kitchen. "I'm so glad you brought food. It's food, isn't it, Daddy? Mommy and I are so hungry and we went to the firehouse first and then Mommy said we should come here to check on you. And then we found Alana."

I walked into the kitchen and set the food on the table. Cindy looked straight ahead, slouched in her chair with arms folded. I went to the cupboard and fumbled with some plates.

"You need to sit down, Sam," Cindy said. She sounded like the chief.

I did sit, a prisoner resigned to his execution. I looked at Cindy, who was not smiling. I looked at Alana, who was smiling big. And her hair was braided in cornrows with little beads on the end.

The beads snapped when she twirled her head. "Like it?"

I tried to figure out an answer that would cause me the least trouble. "Sure."

"Oh, Daddy, I did it. I mean, Mommy showed me, but Alana has such nice hair. It's all bright and pretty. Oh, I wished I had hair like that."

I picked Rae up and plopped her in my lap, figuring it would make it harder for Cindy to punch me.

"Nothing wrong with the hair that God gave you, Rae," Cindy said.

Cindy got up and set the table. I tore open the bag and took the pie out of the box. Alana's eyes opened wide when she looked from the food to Cindy to Rae to me. I reached for a piece of chicken.

Cindy shot me a glare and folded her hands. "God bless this table, O Lord."

Rae set her hands together and pointed her finger to the ceiling. Alana watched, then bounced in her seat when she seemed to understand. She did the same.

"And God bless this company and keep them safe," I said. "Amen."

Cindy passed me the plates and I filled them with chicken and a slice of pie. Alana made cooing sounds and her eyes rolled around in her head. "This is so good."

"Try this," Cindy said, handing Alana a fork. "You ate yet today, child?"

Alana shook her head, her mouth too stuffed to speak.

"I think if you are going to have company, then you should make sure they are taken care of, don't you, Sam?"

"That's why I stopped by Lucy's," I said.

"Oh, so you went to see Lucy?"

"Just for chicken."

"Uh-huh," Cindy said suspiciously.

"Oh, Sam's been really nice," Alana said. "He's helped me with lots of things."

"Really," Cindy said.

"He helped me with my bath."

44

God no, Alana, don't.

"And I got soap in my eyes and he came and rescued me. He showed me the right way to dry myself."

Cindy clenched her teeth. "That's our Sam. He's very hands on."

"Daddy gives me baths, too," Rae said. "He's very gentle." Rae covered her mouth with her hand and giggled. "The only one here that Daddy doesn't give a bath to is you, Mommy."

Cindy waited until she swallowed her food. "It makes me feel cleaner if I do it myself."

Alana went on about how strong and brave I was. Rae agreed enthusiastically. Cindy sat back, nodding along with every word like a hanging judge, asking Alana questions about where she was from and did she have anyplace else to stay. Alana answered in airy generalities.

At nine-thirty, Cindy announced they had to leave. Rae took Alana's hand and walked her to the front door. Before I left the kitchen Cindy made one of those psssst sounds that reminded me of nails on a chalkboard.

I stopped and she slammed her fist into my solar plexus. She drove into me with her shoulder, backing me up against the wall, out of sight of the doorway.

For a skinny woman she sure hit hard.

"Now, Cindy—"

"Sam Carver, you no good son of a bitch. This is a really sweet girl who has no idea what she's getting herself into."

"I wouldn't hurt her—"

She punched me again.

"Hey, why do we have to get rough for?" I said.

"Shut up. This girl is so ignorant that I can't even hate her. You take care of her, you make sure she's fed, you try and find her folks. You got that? Maybe if you do right by her, it'll show that you're really not the son of a bitch you always pretend to be."

"I swear to you—"

She reared back her fist. I covered my midsection. "It's time you start doing some good in your life. This girl thinks your special. You better not let her down."

"I promise," I said, waiting for her to punch me again. Instead she squinched her lips and looked off to the side.

"You ever think there are people in this world who care about you? My God! Our daughter adores you. She thinks her father is Batman." She shook her head. "We were real worried. I wish you would have called."

Cindy held her fists tight at her waist. Her body trembled. She pinched her beautiful lips closed.

"She's just somebody I met, that's all."

"Sure," she squeaked. "You got a way of doing that."

I started to get angry. She was the one who told me I had to leave. Now she wanted to monitor my love life?

"Sam, it's just that—"

"Maybe we should just leave it alone."

She started shaking harder and I thought she was either going to hit me again or break out in tears. But, no, Cindy never cried. She always had to be the one who was right, who did the right thing, and make sure that I knew about it. Instead she snatched her purse off the chair, hurried through the living room, and grabbed Rae's hand.

Rae waved. "Bye, Daddy. Bye, Alana. I love your hair."

Anger sometimes brings moments of clarity, which was why I used drugs. Maybe I needed Cindy to have faith in me. Damn it, I was thrown off a fire truck. I was in pain. I would have straightened things out if she'd just given me more time.

Then came the other chorus. I was a bum. After my accident, I got hooked on the stuff and had to go to rehab. I knew from watching hypes my entire life that those sad people in the streets never ever got better. Druggies lied and stole and finally broke down because most of all they fooled themselves.

Cindy was right to leave me.

***

I slumped on the couch. Alana stood at the window, bobbing up and down, waving enthusiastically as Cindy and Rae drove down the street.

"They are so nice," Alana said, skipping over to the couch and letting her body glide down next to mine. "I just love Rae. I want to do things with her. I bet we could have so much fun. And Cindy, she's so beautiful. Her skin, it's different than yours. Hers shines. She looks like a queen."

I turned to her. I felt like someone had taken a high-pressure hose to the inside of my skull. "I told you not to answer the door."

"I know."

"You answered the door."

She nodded vigorously. "But that was because of Rae. She was so sad. She said, "Daddy, Daddy, I need you. Please, Daddy, tell me you're okay."

My head flopped back and clunked against the wall.

"I couldn't let her be sad."

The Italians could come by any minute and break my legs. I might have to have my father committed to get his power of attorney. My ex had punched me in the gut. Twice.

"You're not mad, are you, Sam?"

And I had a crazy girl in my apartment.

I sat up and took her hand and looked her in the eye. "Alana."

She settled down in her seat, dropped her chin, and tried to play serious. "Sam."

"Look. You're beautiful. You're sexy. It's like you just walked out of a dream."

"It feels like a dream, doesn't it?"

"But it might not be safe for you to stay here. I'm in a lot of trouble and I got stuff to work out."

"Poor Sam."

"Like tonight. I could have worked on my problem." Like I could have called Janice, boned her, and maybe gotten her to lend me a thousand. "Instead, well, we got into other things."

Alana slumped back into the couch. "Oh."

"People don't just fall out of the sky. You had to come from somewhere. Is it that you don't remember?"

She looked down at her lap. "I don't want to talk about it."

"But we have to talk about it. I can't just send you out on the street. You won't let me call somebody who can put you up."

"Please don't do that."

I fought against raising my voice. "You showed up with no clothes. You won't tell me a damn thing about yourself. What if somebody else found you? Somebody except me? This is a rough neighborhood. You could have been hurt."

"I'm lucky to have you," she said quietly.

"Or you could have run into the police. Or walked into a store. They would have called someone. And then they would put you away."

"Please, no."

"Yes. Two white guys with name tags on their suits. They'd say they were from some hospital. And they'd strap you down and take you to a scary place."

She turned pale. For the first time, I saw her composure crumble. She jumped for me, threw her arms around me, and buried her face in my neck. "Don't say it, Sam."

"I'm just trying to show you—"

"You mustn't say things that frighten me."

My God, she was trembling. "Okay, I'll protect you. Don't worry. Just settle down."

"They'll know if I'm afraid. That's how they'll find me. No, Sam, you can't let them. You have to help me."

I took her face in my hands, our noses inches apart. Her green eyes sparkled like emeralds. She shook so much I worried she was going to break apart.

"I'm only saying this because I want to help you."

"You mustn't scare me, Sam."

"Then give me something to work with here."

"Please Sam? I can't say it. Not now. But I need you." Again she dove into my neck. "I need you so very much."

***

Okay, so I have no common sense and I'm a dog. But a green-eyed goddess threw herself at me. Besides Rae, she was the one pure thing I had in my life since—well, for a long time. What else could I do? The Italians could have burst into my bedroom and shot me to pieces and I would have died a happy man. Alana and I didn't have sex; we made love in the most magical way. I was in my bedroom on a mattress with broken springs in a cramped apartment, two months back on the rent, and I couldn't have been happier.

CHAPTER FIVE

I sat up with a start. The streetlights sent silver slivers through the cracks of my curtains. I looked to the end table to the clock. The red numbers said four-o-two.

Alana lay still, like the most beautiful daughter of Midas who fell victim to his touch. Her hair rested on the pillow in coils of spun gold. Her skin was pale and unblemished. A frightening thought came to me and I rested my hand on her chest. She breathed.

I tried to hold on to the wonderful feeling of making love to her. But it slipped through my fingers. My stomach started to cook and my muscles tensed. I'd thought maybe I'd found a little peace. What a joke.

Even the objects in my room seemed to mock me. Like it was my fault the drawer on the dresser stuck, that the wooden chair was wobbly, that the nap of the black velvet in the lion wall hanging looked shiny.

Generally when I tensed up, my back would start to ache. Now it burned in hot pain.

I reached into the nightstand and pulled out my special cigar box. I always kept a few joints pre-rolled so I wouldn't spill grass over the carpet if I fumbled with it in the middle of the night. The flame from the lighter gave a red glow to my fingers.

"Sam?"

I turned to her. "Hey, babe. Be right with you."

She slid over to me and set her hand on my shoulder. "You're suffering."

"Naw. I'll be fine in a minute."

Pain scorched my fingers. I yelped and dropped the Bic. "Shit, Alana, don't get on my case."

"Sam." She didn't raise her voice but there was a clear command to it. "I don't want you to do that."

"Do what? It's just a little dope. Takes the edge off. Helps me sleep."

She reached over me, took the joint from my hand, and set it on the end table. Then she placed her hands on the back of my neck. "I can help you."

"I've been doing this for years."

She ran her hand over the side of my face. "You know, sometimes we have to run. But we should never run from ourselves."

Now she was really getting into my business. I had to set her straight. "Look, Alana—"

"Shhh." She stroked my hair. Her eyes scanned my face. "I know all about it."

Something gave way inside me and crumbled to dust. Something that threatened me. I realized I'd been holding it up in front of me until my arms ached, but now I was tired and it just collapsed. Crazy thoughts I couldn't fully form, jolts of pain, and obscure masses that drifted in dark clouds all seemed to fall apart.

And I was alone and cold and unprotected.

"My poor Sam," she said, wrapping her arms around me. "It's only right. Someone else gets to be the strong one and you have to let them save you. Everything is going to turn out for you."

I remember falling onto the mattress. I never slept so well in my life.

***

The next morning, the Crown Vic glided through the streets of the east side of Buffalo. My dad had this coffee thing at the doughnut shop with a bunch of old guys, so he wasn't home when I stopped by and grabbed a box of my sister's old clothes. Alana liked the green hooded sweatshirt and green leggings because they matched her eyes. The shiny black boots fit well enough. On my sister, they came up to her knees. They made it to mid-calf on Alana. She snatched a black beret and tilted it to one side of her head. My sister's shorts had to be cinched with a belt that I made an extra hole in. Six inches of Alana's creamy skin showed between leggings and shorts.

As we drove, Alana looked around at everything. I noticed a frown pulling down her perfect face.

"What's wrong?"

"I wish it were prettier," she said, leaning her head against the window.

"It's the 'hood, Alana."

"The people are pretty," she said. "I mean, some aren't really beautiful like Cindy and Rae, but they still have pretty looks on their faces. See over there? A bunch of young ones talking like they're friends. That young woman is holding her child's hand. I see lots of good around. I just think they deserve something better."

I looked out at the empty lots strewn with garbage, the sagging houses in need of paint. One driveway had a rusty car resting on blocks.

"Come on," I said. "I'm gonna take you somewhere nice."

She sat up in her seat when we passed Main Street with its century-old mansions of marble or sandstone that now were corporate headquarters or private schools. We took the cross street where homes, out of a 1900s catalog, stood tall. Barely a car length separated each residence. No burn outs here. Elms towered over the houses and curved over the street in a canopy of spiderweb branches. A man wearing a heavy sweater raked leaves off his front lawn.

"This any better?"

"Houses are nicer. People are the same," she said.

I knew of this little coffee shop buried on a side street. I used it when I had to impress a sister with my worldliness. Pulling the car in the rear lot, I grabbed Alana's hand, guided her up the steps, and took a seat a few rows back of the window.

"What should I get?" Alana asked.

"Whatever you want," I said. I had found two twenties in my dad's drawer.

"I want to taste everything!"

With every sip of her peppermint tea and every nibble of a scone, brownie, and oatmeal cookie, she made an "oh" sound. She rolled her head and squeaked when she tasted a parfait.

"Alana, haven't you ever had whipped cream before?"

She looked side to side suspiciously and beckoned me over with her finger. I leaned close and she stuck a dollop on my nose.

"Oh, you're going to pay for that," I said. I grabbed her thin wrists in one hand and scooped some cream with the fingers of the other. She stretched back and moved her head side to side. "You'll never catch me," she said.

I leaned in, dabbed with my fingers. She jerked back and forth. My God, she was fast. She reared her head back and rich laughter serenaded my ears.

Suddenly her face stiffened. Her eyes opened wide and she pushed flat against the wall.

"Alana—"

"Don't move Sam."

"What's wrong?"

"They can't see me, can they?"

"Who?"

"Please help me."

I looked around the restaurant. People ate lunch. Waitresses hurried around. I heard pots clattering in the kitchen.

"Calm down, Alana. Nobody's going to hurt you."

She jerked her head. "They're outside."

I started to turn. "No. Don't let them know you can see them!"

I bent down to tie my shoe, looking casually around the restaurant and out the front window. I didn't see anything wrong. Leaves fell from the trees. Cars stopped at the stop sign and moved on. A few people walked by. Two guys looked at the menu in the front window.

I turned back to her. "Alana, I don't see anything."

"There's two of them," she said.

I looked again, as if I were trying to find the waitress. Everything appeared normal. The two men looked around, stuck their hands in their pockets. Their hair was perfectly combed and they were both trim and good looking. Tall, model types. They exchanged whispers.

"Nothing there except a couple of gay guys," I said.

"What are they wearing?" she said in a low whisper.

"Regular stuff," I said. "Casual suits. Probably don't work downtown, not formal enough." I glanced back their way. "Wait a minute. They each have a name tag. So they probably work at one of the hospitals."

She forced her body hard against the wall. Her lips were stretched over her teeth.

"Alana—"

"Get me out of here, Sam."

I looked out again and the two of them were staring at me. I stared back and they looked down at the street, leaning their heads together. After a second, they walked out of view.

I had great instincts for danger; that served me well as a firefighter. And everything sensible told me there was nothing wrong and my beautiful crazy girl was acting the fool. Every calculation told me this was a regular day and even if it weren't, two skinny dudes weren't going to hurt Alana. Not with me around.

But the back of my neck prickled just like it did when I was in a bad spot in a burning building.

Alana whimpered. The danger was as real to her as a four-alarm fire.

I'd play along. For her.

"Alana," I said, "see that hall? It leads to the rest rooms. There's a rear exit. Put up your hood." She did. "And lean forward. Tuck your hair back. Head that way." I nodded in the direction of the hall. "And stay close to the wall. It's kind of in a shadow. Make like you're going to the bathroom. Go out the door and jump in the back seat. Try and scooch down on the floor."

"But—"

"We got to stay calm. No running. I'm going to pay the check, then meet you in the car."

"I want you to stay with me."

I spoke slowly. "When there is danger, you don't speed up. You tamp things down. In your mind. Make sure you see everything. Make sure you're in the moment."

She nodded quickly.

"Now go."

She threw her hood on, hunched over, and slinked across the wall. I stood up, studied the check, and walked to the register.

"Everything okay?" the waitress asked.

"Just great," I said. As I made change, I studied the room. A bell tinkled when an older couple came through the door. The waitress by the window offered extra coffee to a table of three overweight white men in hunting vests. "Jodie! Order up table four," the cook called from the kitchen.

Alana ducked out the back door.

I followed Alana down the hall and through the door. As if I were enjoying the day, I took out my car keys and looked around, then plopped into the front seat.

"Sam." From the back seat came her thready whisper.

"Everything's fine," I said without turning my head. "I just had lunch and I'm headed back to the 'hood where all good Black people belong. Nothing out of the ordinary."

I did a three-point turn and pulled out into the street, traveling a short block until I rolled to a stop sign.

"Are they gone?"

"You're safe." I checked my rear mirror. The two men in suits sprinted like they knew how down the center of the street. Another oddity in the story of Alana. I pressed on the gas and made a quick turn, then another. Soon I was on the main drag where I took the entrance for the expressway.

The Crown Vic did seventy easily. "Come on up here, Alana," I said. She slid over the bench and leaned against the opposite door.

"Pull your hood down," I said. She did. Her hair unraveled.

"Alana, look at me."

She slowly turned my way. A low whimper came out with her breath.

"Anything you want to tell me?"

She shook her head. "Did you see them?"

"I don't know. I saw two guys in suits. I'm not used to running away from a couple of snowflakes."

She swallowed hard.

She was so frail that I didn't want to yell. But it was time for her to give me some answers. "What are you not telling me? You don't think I'm stupid, do you?"

"No, Sam."

"I mean, this fairy princess act of yours isn't a way to pull something over on me, is it?"

"I told you I'll never lie to you."

"But you won't tell me what's going on, either."

"I can't."

I slammed on the pedal and the Crown Vic roared up to ninety-five.

"Please don't be mad."

"I got to take care of some business. So you're going back to my place. This time you don't answer the door to anyone, okay?"

***

After a shower and a quick call to Janice, I was back on the road. The O'Jays sang "Back Stabbers" on the oldies station. I cursed along with the music.

There was some game going on and I was letting myself get pulled into it. The thing was, I was good at reading people, and I didn't see any tricks in Alana.

I couldn't help Alana if she wouldn't talk to me. And I didn't have time for any of this. Now I had to apply some of that old Sam Carver magic and extract a couple of grand from a lady who had the hots for me.

I made my way down the main drag until I was out of the city. There I slowed down below the speed limit and coasted through the winding turns. When the cops saw a Black man in a big car, they *had* to pull him over. In the suburbs, Driving While Black is a serious offense.

The houses were newer types with double garages and too much lawn for a brother to bother with. I pulled into a driveway that took me to this house that tried to look like an English castle. It had a turret in front and a door under an arch. I looked around for the drawbridge and moat.

I tapped on the door. Janice opened up and greeted me with a big smile that stretched her lipstick. She was tall and trim, almost eye to eye with me in her high heels. Her cocoa-colored skin contrasted nicely with her hazel eyes. She wore a blue dress that clung real nice at those extra wide hips.

"Hey, baby," she said. "I saw the news. You're okay, aren't you? I'm so sorry about the little boy." She took my jacket and leaned in with a maternal smile, then kissed me on the lips in a non-maternal way.

We sat down to dinner. Cooking was one of her many talents. She worked a good job downtown, she had money from her divorce, she was intelligent and driven. And just into her forties. Also, she was desperate for a steady man.

After dinner, we shifted to the couch and drank Hennessy out of expensive looking bell-shaped glasses. She listened to my bullshit like I was saying something important, her eyes opened wide with interest. She was a lot of a woman. But pleasing this type of woman was my specialty.

We emptied our glasses a couple times before she pounced. Her mouth was all over my face, her hands tugged at my shirt. I snapped off the clasp on the back of her dress. She pulled back and wriggled it off over her head.

I dove in, pushing her back onto the cushions. She slithered out of her bra and panties.

Her make-up left a chalky taste in my mouth and her hair felt stiff as wire. I saw the fillings on her teeth when she leaned back and let out a hungry moan. Her nails bit into my back as her hips jerked up to mine.

"Oh, Sam. I'm so ready for you," she said.

I reared up for entry.

Nothing happened.

I concentrated. Some girl had taught me this Zen trick where you tense your lower abdomen and force blood into your dick. I rubbed against Janice. I thought happy thoughts.

Still nothing.

I kept trying. The more she encouraged me, the softer I got. She promised me it would all work out if I just laid back and relaxed and let her go to work. Something quivered inside me and I felt as though any minute I was going to leap out the window. I grabbed my clothes, made my apologies, and hurried the door.

I was so distracted I almost ran a stop sign at the corner of her street. What was I doing? I should have stayed. She was willing to help me work out the kinks. After I had given her a good going over and brought her to a grateful conclusion, I could have gotten a couple grand from her easily.

But I couldn't stand the smell of her deodorant, the stretch lines on her breasts, the way my knees stuck to her leather couch, the ceramic cherubs on the end table that kicked one foot in the air and stared at me with dead eyes. I couldn't have stayed there one more second.

Come on, Carver. You can always find a way. You're always in control.

I felt a softness in my gut like something had drained out of me. Thoughts of fighting with my dad for the power of attorney, bullshitting the Italians, keeping the developers at bay, all of that seemed unimportant.

I drove home as if on autopilot. My life was falling apart.

And I didn't care.

I turned the car off and sat in the driveway. Maybe I had another day before disaster. At least it would be a good day since I'd spend it with Alana.

I walked up the front steps and pulled my keys out. The window overhead slammed open.

"You better keep it quiet down there," a woman shouted at me. I looked up. Mrs. Brown, she of plump face and stringy yellow hair, leaned her head out the window directly over the door.

"Sorry about that." I had no idea what she was talking about.

"I mean it. I pay rent. I don't have to put up with all this pounding," she said.

"It won't happen again," I said. I directed my key to the lock, which was torn away. The door was ajar.

A chill ran through my body. I threw open the door and walked into the house screaming Alana's name.

"This is just what I'm talking about," Mrs. Brown shrieked. "I'm calling the landlord right now."

"Alana, where are you?" I walked into the bedroom to find all of my drawers pulled out and the contents dumped on the floor. I ran to the kitchen and then into the bathroom where the fall breeze ruffled the sheer curtains. The window was opened as far as it goes, about a foot. It was a thin window and only a very thin person could crawl out. I stuck my head through and looked down.

My heart pounded. Who could have smashed open my door? Had those two guys from the restaurant followed us?

Damn it, Alana, why didn't you tell me what was going on?

I ran out the front door, ignoring Mrs. Brown's screeches, and circled around to the back window. On the ground lay a bottle of shampoo. I picked it up and sniffed the honeysuckle scent. Did Alana leave me this as a clue that she had gotten away? If she were chased, she'd go to the rear, not to the street. I trotted through the neighbor's yard towards the fence. There were tracks in the soft dirt. It could have been anybody. But I hopped the low fence and ran desperately into the twilight.

***

The east side of Buffalo is full of lonely places. Stores in need of repairs. Seedy bars that advertised with flickering neon. Abandoned warehouses protected by broken fences and windows secured by warping plywood.

I'd doubled back home and made some calls. Rich and Willie teased me for a minute as I described a missing girl who was nearly six foot tall with golden hair. Eventually my desperation made an impression and they promised to jump in their cars and help with the search. I called a couple of buddies in the police department and they said they'd look around in their patrol cars. As I left the house, Mrs. Brown leaned out the window and shouted, "You're a menace, Carver! The landlord says he's kicking you out."

Slowly, I drove the streets, shining my milk carton-sized firefighting lantern through yards and vacant lots. I vowed that if I caught up with those jerks in suits, I was going to whip them good.

Who are they? What do they want with Alana?

I considered the possibilities and came up blank. It could be anything—because Alana had told me nothing.

I kept driving with a lost cause looking me in the face. Some of these places I hadn't been in since I was a kid. Neglected playgrounds. Railroad tracks lined by tall grass. Most of it had to be searched on foot, and one hundred men couldn't get the job done. The 'hood was the easiest place to get lost in. And if you didn't know your way around, it was the surest place to get hurt.

Willie and Rich had promised to meet me back at the firehouse at eleven. It was a quarter past now, but I just couldn't get off the streets. I crept along, playing the beam of my light over porches and yards. *Please, Alana. Come back to me.*

Ahead of me, a car turned down the street, the headlights momentarily blinding me. From the glare in my rearview mirror, I saw another pair of high beams bearing down and covering the distance between us quickly.

A car door slammed. The tap of shoes on pavement punctuated the night. The bright lights obscured form. I got that hair-standing-on-the-back-of-the-neck feeling. I hesitated and craned my neck out the window.

I saw the black suit, the heavy build. The fucking Italians. I locked the door and furiously cranked up my window and reached for the gear shift. An arm shot through the window opening and a fist slammed me in the temple. Everything swayed. When things cleared a bit, I found myself ass on the pavement and leaning against my door. I looked up at three of Big Sal's guys.

"Hey, Victor," I said. "Kind of late for you guys to be out in the 'hood."

He leaned over and whacked me on the side of the head with the flat of his hand. I saw stars.

"I got to tell you, Sam, Sal's kind of worried."

"Sal's so fat he'll worry himself into a heart attack," I said.

Slam. More stars. "Fellas, if you keep hitting me like this," I said, "I'm not going to be able to carry on a conversation."

"Kinda past the time for conversation, Sam. And we're kinda fed up with your lip," Victor said. He nodded to the men on either side. Two paws grabbed my jacket and I bobbed up like a marionette.

"Please, Vic. I just need some more time."

"You need a strong reminder," he said. He bent down and smashed his fist into my stomach. I felt a jolt through my entire nervous system. "Sorry, Sam. I got to take a piece of you this time."

I spit up bile. "If you hurt me, I won't be able to work."

"Just following orders. Sal said you were quite the football star back in the day. Quarterback, right? Tell me, did you throw righty or lefty?"

"Please guys, no."

Victor nodded and the two big lugs grabbed my right arm.

"One by one, we're gonna take things from you. You don't want to get to the point where you don't have at least one good arm to function with. Pretty hard to make good like that."

One man wrapped his arm around my neck and slammed my cheek against the car hood. I tried to struggle, but he had leverage and was too strong. The other took my right arm and stretched it out so that the edge of the quarter panel was the fulcrum and my arm was the teeter-totter. Victor reached under his coat; in the light from the high beams, I saw a small, thick club.

"Look, guys. I was just going to the firehouse. I got a few hundred there. It's better than nothing. You won't have to go back empty handed."

"I wish you wouldn't insult my intelligence," Victor said, stepping forward, slapping the club against his palm.

Brakes screeched. Lights glared from the front and two more doors slammed. Victor got a puzzled look on his face. The guy who held my arm let go and flipped open the buttons on his coat. I saw the black steel of his holstered thirty-eight.

The steps came closer. "Who the fuck is it," Victor yelled.

A voice came from the front of my car, hidden by the high beams. "I guess you guys must not know what neighborhood you're in." Willie stepped into the light. His shoulders hunched over, letting his leather jacket dangle down in front of him. This wasn't the tired old firefighter who spent his nights watching old westerns and padded around the firehouse in his slippers. His face looked like a map to hell.

Victor stood up straight. "Yeah? Well, who the fuck are you?"

"We're his friends," Rich said, stepping into the light, wearing a cut off sweatshirt that couldn't contain his shoulders. He'd never looked this scary before, with the headlights blanching out his face like weathered stone. "So maybe you should get your fucking hands off of him."

"He owes us," the guy holding me said. He yanked back on my neck. I thought I was going to pass out.

Rich moved fast, grabbing the man's wrist and shrugging him back to the rear of the car. Victor reached into his coat for his gun.

"You better think twice," Willie said. He flipped open his coat to show the silver forty-four tucked in his belt.

"I don't answer to no fucking eggplants," Victor said. He put his hand on his pistol. Willie was quicker, snatching his gun out of his belt and planting it under Victor's nose.

"Motherfucker," the third guy said, reaching for Willie's arm. Rich threw a quick jab into his solar plexus and the man went down.

"This is Big Sal's business," Victor said, pulling his hand away and leaving his gun in the holster. "This one," he pointed to me, "owes us."

"I understand that," Willie said, slipping his gun back into his belt. "But you're in our house now. How would you like it if we came over to your neighborhood and brought down some shit down?"

"You're getting yourself in deep," Victor said.

"Maybe," Willie said. "But do you want to go back to Big Sal and say you got into a shooting war with the brothers? And maybe I got another five with shotguns waiting in the bushes."

Victor looked around nervously.

"You know how hard it is to see us at night," Willie said.

Victor tugged on his coat, snapped his fingers, and pointed to the car. The two other guys walked back. "You got the upper hand. This time. But this keeps getting worse. There will come a time when he can't hide behind you."

The three big Italians skulked back to their car. "Tell Big Sal I'll call him," I shouted. "Sorry about this, Victor. It's all gonna work out."

Victor glared at me over his shoulder, then got into the car. With the screech of rubber, they were gone.

"I'm really fucked," I said.

"Probably," Willie said. "But I don't think they'll tell Big Sal what just happened. It'd just make them look bad."

Willie slumped and looked old and tired again. Rich shook his head.

"Guys, I don't know what to say," I said.

"We got your back, Sam," Rich said.

"The motherfucking Turk." Willie cackled. "Straighten this shit out or we're all gonna get killed."

He grabbed my arm and led me back to his car. Rich opened up the back door. From the dark interior, one black boot stepped down. Green leggings ran down to her knee. Two long arms stretched out. Pale graceful hands grabbed the frame. The black beret sat on the side of her head. Alana's face had a sad, sheepish look.

She stood up. I grabbed her and held her head against my shoulder.

I looked from Willie to Rich. "Goddamn, I love you guys," I said.

"She was hiding behind the trash cans at the firehouse," Rich said.

"I'm so sorry, Sam," she said. "I've been a lot of trouble, haven't I?"

CHAPTER SIX

Rich took Alana to one of his apartments near the University of Buffalo. He said the downstairs tenant was a little Polish lady who watched the neighborhood like a sheriff. I was in a lot of trouble and I didn't want Alana to end up a casualty. Plus, I needed her in a safe place so I could do what I had to do.

Alana protested, but finally said if I wanted her to go, she would. Because she knew I would never let her down.

Willie and I took my car back to the firehouse. At the kitchen table, he went to the cabinet, pulled out the bottle covered by the paper bag and tipped a shot into each of our coffee cups.

"You want one, Joe?" Willie offered. Joe was a heavy-set white guy with receding hair and hips that gave him the shape of a pear. He worked the captain's crew.

"I'm good, Willie," Joe said. "Just don't make too much noise. The captain's a light sleeper." He walked out the kitchen door that led to the apparatus floor.

I leaned over my cup and sipped. The bourbon stung my throat but warmed my stomach.

"You are a trip, Sam."

"I thought you were back in your old gang banger days," I said. "I don't know what I would have done without you guys."

"You would have gotten your ass whipped," Willie said. "Would it help if I told you that you better get your fucking shit together?"

"Probably not."

We settled in to a couple of long sips. Then Willie spoke. "You want to tell me how it happened?"

"I had some deals going. I thought everything would work out."

"I know your kind of deals. Betting on ball games. Shooting craps. You're always going to be a fuck up when it comes to money. I'm talking about the girl."

I smiled. "She just showed up." I told him how I met Alana.

Willie shook his head. "Don't this seem strange to you, cous? A girl that fine just falling into your lap?"

"She was in trouble."

"Oh, I can see the trouble all right." Willie sighed. "Someday all the sisters you've been fucking are gonna turn on you. Then you can forget about Big Sal because you'll really have to run for your life."

I smiled. I remembered the way Alana looked when she went into the car before Rich drove her away. Her eyes were like green beacons. She'd looked at me with her puppy dog face and said, "I know you won't let me down."

Joe stuck his head in the kitchen. "Sam, someone at the door for you."

I looked at Willie. He stood up and unzipped his coat. The handle of the forty-four slid forward.

"Who is it, Joe?"

"I don't know. Two guys in suits."

Spitting angry, I threw out every curse I knew and rushed for the door. Willie set his hand on my chest. "They got some big balls to come over here after they smashed my door," I said.

"Now, don't go rushing into more trouble. Just chill out and listen to what they have to say."

I walked through the apparatus floor. I heard Willie's footsteps behind me.

Through the crack in the door, I saw the two men admiring themselves like supermodels. "Sam Carver?" one said. He was dressed in a pale suit with a name tag on his lapel. The man next to him was just as tall and thin and dressed the same way.

I swung the door open and stepped toward them. I held my fists at my waist. I ached to drive my knuckles into their pretty faces. "Who the fuck are you?"

The men looked at each other. Then one said, "I believe you might have gotten the wrong impression. My partner and I work at an exclusive clinic. We need to speak with you about the girl you are harboring. In private, please."

I looked back at Willie. He shrugged.

"Okay," I said. "Go around to the parking lot."

***

I sat behind the wheel of my Crown Vic, looking at the mirror at the two odd men in my back seat.

Now I saw why I thought they were gay. They were perfect. Almost beautiful. Their hair, two different shades of brown, shone even in the dome light of my car. Their faces were long and angular. They were neatly, even perfectly, shaven. Not one blemish marked their skin.

"This better be good," I said, "because you fucking broke my door."

"Mr. Carver," the one on the passenger side said, "I hope I can clear things up for you. The girl you are harboring, well, she comes from a

62

prominent family."

"Alana," I said.

"That is not her real name," he said.

"So who is she?"

"I would prefer to protect the confidentiality of our client, who would be the guardian of the girl in question. Let's just call this girl Jane Doe."

"I'm listening."

"Three days ago, on her way to vacation at an aunt's house, Jane escaped by jumping off a train."

The train tracks did run through the neighborhood and Amtrak had a midnight run.

"You make it sound like she was a prisoner."

"She's not well, Mr. Carver, and she needs constant supervision. We found her clothes a short distance from the tracks. We believe she shed them to escape identification. Jane's family has position and wealth. And they desire anonymity."

"Come on, guys," I said. "How many rich people take the train anymore?"

The two men exchanged a glance. "Among many other more serious mental problems, Jane has a fear of flying."

The other spoke, "Jane has been seemingly stable for a long time. Those who attended to her let their guard down."

"She came to the firehouse door wearing nothing but a stolen fire coat," I said.

"It's not the first time some such thing has happened. Jane's mother loves her too much to institutionalize her. But she very much desires her return."

"What if Alana—Jane—doesn't want to go back?"

"That would be unfortunate. We are not kidnappers, Mr. Carver. But our client is Jane's legal guardian. If we are unsuccessful, it is likely that the authorities might step in and order her confined in a facility. It would distress our client if Jane is not returned home safe and sound. And most importantly, it would not be in Jane's interest."

"So you're so sure you know what her interests are?"

"What do you think?" the other man leaned close to the front seat. "How do you find her behavior? Is she stable or erratic? Can she take care of herself? Would she be liable to meet the wrong people and fall into trouble?"

I looked down and said quietly, "I can take care of her." I thought of her on that first night, how fragile she was.

"Mr. Carver, you will forgive us for being thorough. But your current position is not the most stable. In view of what took place earlier this evening, it seems that anyone around you might be subjected to violence."

"I'll be all right."

"That may very well be true. You seem to be a man of substantial ingenuity. But the point is, are you sure that Jane will be all right?"

"Our client is very grateful you were the one Jane ran into. As you can imagine, she might not have been so lucky if the wrong person found her."

"We need you to tell us where she is, so we can take her home where she will be safe."

"You want me to rat on her?"

"We want you to do what's in Jane's best interest," the first one said. "She needs professional help, and that is more than you can provide."

"We're asking you to do the right thing. For Jane."

"Fuck," I said. I ran my palm over my head. I was drawn to Alana. I wanted to protect her. I wanted her next to me. She made me feel better. But what could I actually give her, especially considering her condition?

"Our client is prepared to show her gratitude," the second one said. He picked up his briefcase and brought it up to seat level. The clasp snapped open, he pried back the lid, and there before me sat a shitload of money.

"Wow."

"Fifty thousand dollars. And all we want is an address so we can help Jane."

A few inches away was the solution to all my problems, with enough money left over to take care of Cindy and Rae. Hell, they deserved it, didn't they? Didn't I deserve a new start? I could make good with Sal. I wouldn't have to pressure my dad for his property.

And Alana—I mean Jane—would be better off back home.

"I just don't know."

"Mr. Carver, I wish we had plenty of time to allow you to decide. But if you choose not to cooperate, we may have to involve our other assets."

"What assets?"

"The police, for one. Jane has a court appointed guardian because of her mental deficiencies. If you keep her from us, you might be subject to certain legal actions. Criminal and civil."

"Are you threatening me?"

"We are speaking plainly. Our client loves Jane. She has unlimited assets and intends to bring her back home."

The money was bundled with rubber bands. The bills were worn and different denominations. Untraceable. I had to admire their thoroughness.

"Our intention is to help Jane," the first man said. "And we will do so, one way or another. The only question is are you willing to help her, too?"

***

Some things you just have to be alone for. I gave Willie some vague answer about what the two men wanted. He shot me a suspicious look and, after a while, left for home.

My cup was filled halfway with Willie's whiskey. I'd finally done the right thing, I told myself. I gave them the address; they gave me the money. I tucked the suitcase in my trunk.

Alana, or Jane, was obviously nuts. Showing up naked. Her act with the shampoo. It was all because she was a disturbed person looking for attention.

How silly she'd looked at the window, tapping her finger at a spider, displaying her beautiful self for all to see, without a care in the world. I didn't think I could ever forget that. I looked across the table to the chair where she first sat, where she ate with her hands and cobbler dribbled down her chin.

How she threw her arms around me and kissed me.

Crazy stuff.

I thought of her innocent eyes, the strangest, brightest green I'd ever seen, how they'd shone like pools of tranquility when she told me she trusted me.

Stop it, Sam.

I took another swallow.

I told myself again that I had done the right thing.

Then why did my stomach burn?

I looked at the clock. Quarter after twelve. It was a ten-minute drive to the apartment. Alana was now safe in their custody. They'd probably given her the proper medications and she was snoozing in the back seat of a limo on her way back to her mom.

From the radio, the dispatcher announced that Engine 27 was finishing up a call. It was Mona's address. Could have been a drunk making trouble or maybe Buddy had to crack someone on the side of the head. Then I heard the call for the coroner.

I jumped up, grabbed the department phone. "Hey, this is Sam Carver from Engine 39. That call on Pierce Street. Why did they send homicide over there?"

"It's was a mess, Sam. Forced entry. Two people were killed."

"Shot?"

"Beaten to death."

"Who?"

"Well, the lady who owned the place, for one. You know Mona Fredrick? She runs numbers. Engine 27 said there wasn't much left of her. And some big guy."

I slammed the phone down and dropped into my seat. Everyone in the 'hood knew that Mona had money, but getting to her was another matter. She kept a three-fifty-seven on her hip, a twenty-two on her ankle. And you would have needed a torpedo to get through Buddy.

Something else to turn my stomach. Mona and Mom went way back. Sure, she didn't lend me money, but who in their right mind would?

Absently, I picked up the stack of newspapers in the center of the table and flipped through them. Scouting report from last week's Bills game. A crossword puzzle that somebody had already filled out. A coupon page clipped to shreds. Couldn't we at least get today's paper?

I looked through the USA Today and snickered at the coincidence. Another girl, also from a prominent family, had jumped off the train. But this happened in California. I read on. She had a history of mental problems and, although she was of age, her mother was her legal guardian.

I stood up and slammed the palms of my hands on the table. The woman, who the paper referred to as Jane Doe, threw off her clothes to escape recognition. Under the text was a picture of a dark-haired young woman struggling against the police as she was forced into an ambulance.

The same fucking story. It was like someone had read this before they met me.

I picked up the paper, wadded it into a ball, and threw it against the wall. This was all wrong. The two supermodel dudes were wrong. Why did they still wear their name tags at night? Why were they as perfect looking as … as perfect as Alana herself?

I had a suitcase with fifty grand in my trunk, given to me on the same night Mona was robbed and murdered.

It all started to piece together.

The clock said twelve sixteen. Plenty of time for them to pick her up and drive her to God knows where.

But I hadn't seen a car. That didn't make any sense. None of this did. If they were on foot, it would take them forty minutes to get to Alana. Maybe less, considering how fast I'd seen them run.

And if they had no car, they weren't taking her anywhere.

Alana, what have I done to you?

I shot through the door shoulder first and ran through the apparatus floor. Joe sat in the phone booth, his legs stretched out the door, phone cradled under his ear.

"Joe, I need the phone right now."

"Give me a minute, Sam. It's my wife."

I reached in and grabbed him by the shirt and yanked him out. "Joe, I am so sorry," I said.

"What the fuck—"

I cut him off when I slammed the door. The overhead light came on; I dropped a quarter into the slot and dialed.

The phone rang and rang. "Pick up, damn you."

After twenty rings, I heard a cheerless voice. "This better be fucking important," Rich said.

"Rich, is there a phone at Alana's?"

"The dead-beat tenants never paid the bill," he said.

"Any way to get in touch with her?"

"Sam, it's after midnight."

My mind raced. Rich lived a few blocks down from where Alana stayed. "How long would it take you to get there?"

"I don't know. Less than ten minutes."

"Rich, I need you to do something."

"You having some sort of break down over there, Sam?"

"Son of a bitch, Rich. Alana's in big trouble. Can you get over there?"

"You serious?"

"Dead serious."

"Is it gonna get rough?"

"I'm not sure. It might."

"Okay. I'm bringing my shotgun with me."

"I'll meet you there."

***

I stomped on the accelerator. The V-8 growled and the Crown Victoria chewed up pavement as I streaked through red lights.

Everything was wrong. Guys with suitcases of money and name tags who smashed doors and plagiarized the USA Today. The most beautiful girl in the world who was a dead ringer for Farrah Fawcett and made love like a five-hundred dollar prostitute but didn't know how to dry herself or use shampoo. And one stupid ex-football star and wannabe hero who was so self-absorbed he let himself fall for the whole pile of shit.

I had failed Cindy and Rae. I had failed little George. I had drawn my two best friends into something I should have kept to myself: my debt to Fat Sal.

If I'd caused Alana harm, I couldn't live with myself. If I lost her, it would be better for me to ram into the side of a building at sixty miles an hour.

Save the self-pity for later. It's time to fly faster than a speeding bullet.

If Rich could get there in time, he could handle those two and five more like them. Plus I had woken him up. It was never good to wake up Big Daddy.

The ride seemed to take forever, even though it was only a few miles. Students lined up on the sidewalk to enter the college bars. A lazy sea of headlights drifted toward me. I was sure that every car that put on a left-hand turn signal did so to deliberately slow me down. I hit the horn at the trim young sister in a long white coat and stiletto heels who dared to cross the street.

When I came to the block where Alana was staying, I screeched around the corner. Two-story doubles lined both sides, each with a postage stamp lawn, a brick front, and a small front porch. When I spotted the house number, I drove up on the lawn. My breath hissed out in relief when I saw Rich's car parked in the driveway. Let's see them get by him.

I took the steps four at a time all the way up to the second-floor door. Inside, the couch laid on its side and the cushions were tossed around the room. Bits of the glass top of the coffee table were scattered over the carpet. I looked down. Rich lay at my feet.

I screamed from the bottom of my soul. "Alana!"

A low groan answered. Rich stirred and used his thick arms to push himself up to a sitting position. I bent down next to him and ran my hands over his neck and shoulders to see if anything was broken.

"Stop it." He shrugged me off. "I'm all right."

"What happened?"

"You didn't tell me they were ninjas. They came barging through the door. I'm waiting for them, my pump at my waist. I'm about to say some Dirty Harry shit, like 'make my day, motherfuckers', and one of them snatches my shotgun from my hands before I could move." Rich pointed to the floor where the gun barrel was snapped from the stock. "He smashes it over his knee like it's a ruler, not a four-hundred dollar Remington twelve gauge. I told them, oh, no, you didn't just do that, you're in trouble now, and I lunged for them, and, Sam, I'm so sorry, all I saw was fists and feet and I had all I could do to keep them off me."

"Where's Alana?"

"While I was getting my ass kicked, she ran out the front door. Damn, that girl is fast. I was wrestling with them and she jumps right over us. They turn to her, forgetting about me. I slid in front of the door and held my arms from one end of the frame to the other. At least that's what I did until I passed out. I swear they must have hit me a hundred times. I'm so sorry about this, Sam."

I patted his shoulder. "You did good, Rich."

I ran out the front porch and looked both ways down the street. The right led to the main road to the college. Would be a good way for Alana to get lost. The left went straight down into the rows of houses. If you made a right a few hundred feet down, you'd turn into an abandoned industrial park.

I ran back to Rich. He looked up at me. A cut on his forehead leaked onto his eyelid and trickled down his cheek.

"I hate to bring this up at a time like this," he said, "but who the fuck is gonna pay for my shotgun?"

"You still have that viewfinder on you?"

"Why? You feel like looking at some titties?"

"Come on," I said. He reached into his pocket. I took it and ran back on the porch.

Locking my leg over the railing, I leaned right towards Main Street. The viewfinder gave me a precise, if narrow, field of sight. I followed the sidewalk; one side, then the other. A couple of students strolled with books in their hands. An old lady pushed her laundry in a cart.

To the left, I followed the sidewalk toward the industrial park. Down one side of the street, all I could see was a guy walking his dog. I scanned the other side. The streetlights provided the only light and there was an area between them that their illumination didn't reach. I moved the viewfinder slowly.

I thought I saw two figures under a lamp post, but they were quickly obscured by the darkness. I moved it up to the next lamp. I saw them again, tall and graceful, hauling their skinny butts fast. I scanned ahead of them. Another figure ran, her golden hair shimmering as she passed under a streetlight. She made a quick right turn and disappeared into the service road of the industrial park.

She was still safe. But for how long?

I turned and ran, sidestepping Rich.

"Cousin, you can't do this alone," he said. "Look what they did to me."

"No time," I called back to him.

My car kicked up dirt. The wheels spun, then caught, and I lurched onto sure pavement. With my high beams on, I searched the sidewalk. If I caught those two passing a driveway, I was going to run them over.

I made it to the industrial park entrance. The parking lot had become a junkyard of old tires, abandoned autos, and upturned pavement. A rectangular four-story brick bordered the left. On the right, protected by a broken fence, lay man-sized spools of cable and pyramids of rotting pallets as tall as a house. A hundred yards down, there was a seven-story building shaped like a shoe box set on its end. The side facing me was in the shadow of the quarter moon, but I could still make out a mane of gold two stories up, following the path of the fire escape. Only Alana had hair like that.

My high beams caught two graceful figures a few yards from the building.

They had her trapped.

The Crown Vic made way in a series of lurches and stops. At fifty yards from the tower, I jumped out. The moon played on her hair of gold as she stepped over the rampart onto the roof.

No sign of the two men. Most of the building was in shadows.

I jumped out of the car and sprinted, sidestepping broken fencing, wending around empty fifty-five-gallon barrels, avoiding potholes where I might land awkwardly and throw out my back or twist my ankle. My breath hummed. I pumped my arms and my clenched fists.

I stopped at the bottom of the ladder and clamped my hands on the cold railings, my chest heaving, sweat dripping from my face. From this position, I could see that the men were rounding the last landing, swallowing the steps like they were rested and hadn't run all the way from the firehouse and beaten Big Daddy into a heap.

I yanked with my arms. My legs churned. Where the men glided up, I pounded, rattling the metal steps. The entire fire escape vibrated. The bolts that held the stairs to the building jerked with each step. I wondered how much they could take before they pulled free. At the third landing, I cursed myself for not keeping up my cardio. At the fifth, I lamented that I'd let myself gain that extra fifteen pounds. I stopped to catch my breath. The two men were out of sight.

I pushed on. My chest felt like I'd just fought a five-alarm fire by myself. I forced my breath out and drew in as much as I could, but I craved more. I needed to stop and lean against the building and suck up the cool night air.

When I made it to the sixth-floor landing, I heard her scream. I saw red, I saw God, I saw stars. I don't know how I did it, but all of a sudden, my legs had strength again and I flew up the rest of the stairs and hurled my body over the parapet. I rolled and the stones on the roof cut through my jeans and into the skin on my hip.

In the middle of the roof stood a stairwell tower. To either side, it was about thirty feet to the ledge. The roof was scattered with debris: rusty cans of roofing patch, a rotted wooden ladder, piles of ropes and cables. The quarter moon peeked over the ledge, making the scene a horror movie of silver and long shadows.

One man stalked slowly at one side of the tower, one at the other. They stretched out their spider arms almost from tower to ledge so that nobody could pass.

On the far end stood Alana, her ankles against the low parapet, so gracefully airy that she looked like she could fly into the moonlight. She sobbed hopelessly.

She drew out my name as if it were a prayer. "Sam?"

I charged. The men turned as one. They exchanged a nod, then one strode purposefully toward me. I wound up to swing for his head. Before I could bring my hand past my ear, his hand shot out, fingers first, landing in my gut. The air hissed out of me and I fell to my knees. Shock waves coursed through my nervous system. I fought to see, but all my brain could process was multicolored exploding stars. I expected a rain of blows from the ninja with a name tag, but they never came. I couldn't tell how much time had passed before my head cleared enough to see Alana darting left, then right, and the two of them cutting off the distance between her.

I grabbed my knees and pushed myself up, stumbling at first. I tripped on a coiled rope, one end of which was tied to an iron hook. I steadied myself and moved forward. Leaning against the tower was a two by four, cut down to maybe four feet. I grabbed it tight. A splinter stung the palm of my hand. The soggy old wood weighed three times as much as it should.

Alana pivoted and tried to shoot between them, but she lost her footing on the gravel and fell to her hands and knees. They were on her, hands under her shoulders and clamped on her wrists. She kicked at them and threw her head back and forth helplessly.

I brought all my anger into that soggy board and cracked it down on the closest one's shoulder. It made a sickening squawk and sunk into his collar bone. His grip on Alana went limp and his left arm seemed to ratchet down about eight inches. They both turned to me in unison, the second one retaining his grip on Alana's wrist. She pulled back and scratched at his hand.

The guy who I'd hit, who should have been on the ground writhing in agony with his shoulder shattered, turned to me. There was no pain on his face. Just hate.

"Take the girl," the other one said. The man with one functioning arm grabbed hold of Alana's wrist. The other one locked eyes on me and stepped forward.

I swung again. With one hand, he caught the board in mid-air, yanked it from me, and flung it over the side of the roof. I guess I should have brought my hands up quicker, but it was one punch after another. If I protected my face, he hit me in the stomach. If I bent over, he slammed me in the back of the neck. The stars spun above me, the asphalt deck rolled, and I fell on my back side.

Alana shrieked, "Leave him alone!"

The guy who'd pounded me senseless looked at her over his shoulder and spoke through his twisted mouth. "Before you die, you get to watch what we do to him."

He stood over me with a backdrop of dark sky and stars, the moon outlining his face in bone white.

"Just let her go, okay?" I said. It didn't make any sense, but I had to try. "Do whatever you want to me. Please don't hurt her."

He shook his head. "You're hardly worth the bother." He took off his sports jacket and threw it to the side.

Out of the corner of my eye, I saw Alana running her hand over the ground. The man whose shoulder I'd fucked up stared down at me in pain-free amusement. Blood soaked through the left side of his jacket.

Alana snatched something, brought it up behind her ear and then jabbed it as hard as she could.

He drew back his hand and looked down at it resentfully. He grabbed the spike in his teeth and removed it from the meaty part of his forearm.

I wished she would have run for the tower and down the stairs, but she ran for me, sliding down beside me, cradling my head, tears running down her cheeks.

"I'm so sorry I got you in this, Sam." She looked over her shoulder. "Leave him alone. It's me you want."

The man grabbed her hair, twisted it in his hand, and yanked her head back. "You don't get to choose." He dragged her toward the side of the roof. She wailed. Stones flew as she kicked her feet.

The man with the broken shoulder walked up to me and kicked me in the ribs. I must have flown back six feet. I tried to protect myself when he kicked again. Out of the corner of my eye, I saw the other man dragging Alana to the edge. She scratched at his face.

Another kick came and I flew again and thumped on the roof. A pain stabbed into my upper back. At least I hadn't hit my tailbone, which might have locked up my lower back but good. I looked up and he strode towards me. I turned on my stomach and tried to push up. Under my nose was the coil of rope I'd tripped over earlier. The stabbing pain I felt came from a hook of maybe six inches in diameter that was tied to the end of the rope.

He wound up for another kick. I rolled and grabbed his other leg and pulled up with all my strength. He went down. I drove my boot against the side of his head. I would have liked to keep stomping until I'd made a paste out of his brain, but I had to save Alana. I reached down for the hook and ran for her.

The other one held Alana with one hand on her arm, one under her throat, as he backed her to the ledge. Her toes fluttered against the stones on the roof. Her face was forced and not a sound escaped as he clamped down on her windpipe.

Her ankles bumped into the ledge. I saw the sneer on the side of his face, the tendons on his neck, her hand limply pawing the front of his coat. Darting forward, dragging the rope behind me, I brought the hook up and sunk it deep in the side of his neck.

Alana dropped and clutched her throat, then coughed convulsively. The man pivoted like a slowly, with choppy steps, until he faced me. Dark blood spit out of his throat around the spike. He brought his hand up weakly and mouthed words without sound.

I heard shuffling. I turned. The other man, with one bad arm and now a smashed jaw, moved quickly toward me, grabbing me by the throat before I could move. His hand made a perfect fit on either side of my windpipe right where I knew my carotid arteries to be. I wriggled. I pounded down on his arm. The blood flow to my brain was being cut off as he squeezed. I felt light-headed and weak. I reached out for his face, but his arm was longer than mine.

"Time to die," he slurred out of his crooked mouth.

I grabbed his wrist with both hands. I kicked at his body. It was like hitting a wood plank. I was seconds away from losing everything, from letting everybody down. I set one foot on his leg and ran up on him, then wrapped my arms and legs over his arm, dropping all my weight. He fell hard on his broken side. Allowing myself one deep breath, I snatched the rope and was on him, curling it once, twice around his neck. He slapped at my hands with his good arm. I leaned back like I was pulling an oar. His legs pushed against the roof, forcing him against me in a desperate attempt to slacken the rope. I leaned again, twisting, hemp burning my hands. My arms ached. Even like this, he was stronger than me. With my last reserve, I forced myself to stand, bringing his head up under my chin, the coarse rope cutting into my hands.

He got his legs under himself for another push, obviously not tired and oblivious to any physical pain. He lurched at me. I dropped to my butt and he rolled over me and fell off the ledge. The rope slithered after him until it pulled taunt. The hook was still embedded in the other one's neck; he shuffled heavy-legged to the ledge. I ducked below the level of the rope and watched him follow his partner.

CHAPTER SEVEN

Seven stories down, there were consecutive explosions that lit up the tall grass and rubbish on the side of the building. Two geysers of dirt followed. Then the dirt settled, and the side of the building was lit only by the moon.

I crawled over to Alana, the stones biting my knees and palms. She steadied herself on all fours and gulped. Tears stained her cheeks. She looked at me sideways, her green eyes, and leaned her forehead against mine. I stroked her, ran my hands over her arms, shoulders, and spine to make sure that everything about her was still perfect. We said nothing as I helped her up. I covered her with my arm. We leaned on each other as we avoided the junk on the roof and made our way to the stairs.

The inside stairs were made of wood and open to each floor. We steadied ourselves with the two-by-four railings. Everything creaked but seemed sturdy enough. The moonlight shone through the tall empty window openings. Each floor we passed was filled with debris: stacks of newspapers, six-foot bins filled with wood shavings, bundles of straw, and old barrels containing God knew what.

At ground level, she tugged at me in the direction of the car. I told her I needed to check something and led her around the side of the building. On the ground, I found the rope with the hook attached and two sets of clothes. I kicked through them and even found tighty whities.

But no trace of the bodies.

I looked for tracks. Under each set of clothes there was a small crater surrounded by scorched grass. Alana stood near the corner of the building, her arms wrapped around her shoulders, her golden hair covering her face.

"You wouldn't by any chance know where they are?" I called to her.

"They're gone," she said, then turned and walked to the car.

The wind carried the sounds of distant traffic. I shuffled after her, taking in deep breaths, rubbing my chafed throat, hobbling as the soreness took hold through my ribs and back. Alana didn't look at me as she opened the passenger door and slid in.

I couldn't wait to get out of there. The rear tires kicked up dirt and I circled around back to the street.

It was as if I'd been in a nightmare and awakened with a start. I had to force myself to focus on the pavement, to remind myself that the parked cars and houses were real. My mind worked hard trying to explain exploding men who felt no pain and what connection they had to Alana. Damn, I had just saved her pretty ass and she wanted to give me the silent treatment? Maybe a fuse blew in my brain at that point; I slumped down in my seat and settled into numbness.

"Alana."

I looked over. She leaned her head against the window, her face hidden by her hood, her fist pulling down on the draw strings.

"Sam."

"You know you have to tell me."

"I can't."

Gathering my thoughts, I made the turn down Main Street. "I'll drive around for a few minutes. But I have to check on Rich. I have to know what to say to him."

"Can you take me somewhere else?"

"I'm running out of hideouts."

I drove absent-mindedly, slowing down long before we came to the red lights, stopping to let pedestrians cross the street.

"A friend of mine is dead," I said.

She turned to me, a portrait of surprise, eyes opened wide, and her face turned pale.

"She was an old lady. Knew my family from way back. Kinda worked on the other side of the law."

"I'm so sorry."

"Somebody robbed her place."

"That's terrible."

"I think those guys we danced with on the tower did it. Seeing how strong they were, they could have easily handled an old lady, even her bodyguard."

She just nodded.

"I'm not going to raise my voice, Alana. I'm just going to say you have to tell me. You've brought me into this. I've protected you. One of my friends is dead, another one is hurt. And two motherfuckers tried to kill us and fell off a seven-story building and exploded like firecrackers. So no matter how hard it is for you, it's very hard for me, too."

"I understand," she said, looking down into her lap. I waited, unsure if she was going to answer. Finally she raised her head, pushed back her hood, and wiped her face with her sleeve. "I'm not from around here, Sam."

That was a start. "Where are you from?"

"Far away."

"Okay." I waited, but she only stared straight ahead. "Is it in New York State?" She shook her head.

"In the United States?"

"Further than that."

I never liked playing twenty questions. "Can you point to it on a map?"

Again she shook her head. "You don't understand, Sam. My people, we've been through this before. When we tell, well, people like you can't accept it."

"You think all us brothers are dumb?"

"Not just Black people. Any of you."

"Any of us who, exactly?"

"People on Earth."

I nodded slowly. "So you're saying you are from a different place than Earth?"

"Something like that."

A bell donged in my head, back and forth, drowning out any rational thought. "Well, that has to be a yes or no answer. I mean, you either are from Earth, or you are not. I know. Maybe you have some Earth relatives and you spend summers here because you like the beach, then go back to your second home, which is—where did you say it was?"

"Ladallia."

I slapped the steering wheel. "There you go. Now it makes sense. All you had to say was Lavedia."

"Ladallia."

"That's right. All you had to say is, Sam, I'm not from Earth. I'm from Ladallia. It would have saved a lot of confusion. And your friends who wore name tags and blew up like Roman candles? I should have pegged them for Ladallians right away."

"Are you okay, Sam?"

I turned to her and swatted the backrest to my right with the side of my arm. Compulsively, I started to grin. I must have looked crazy, because I was stretching the sides of my face and it hurt my lips. "I'm fine. You are from outer space. I slept with a girl who is not human. I killed two guys, but hey, that's okay, because they weren't guys at all. They were from Ladallia. Hell, I can't be arrested for killing two guys from Ladallia."

She looked down at her hands. "This is why we don't like to tell you people."

"Listen, bitch, don't you dare call me 'you people!'"

A horn blared behind me. I looked back. A car missed side-swiping me by inches because I had drifted into his lane. That didn't stop me from rolling down my window, giving him the finger and calling his mama a dirty whore.

I felt her hand on my forearm. I jerked away. I sped down Main Street, whipping past Colonial style mansions of the University of Buffalo campus. The traffic light at the city line had been yellow for an entire second when I gunned it. Someone was about to make a left; they slammed on their brakes and hit their horn.

I drove twenty miles an hour over the speed limit, hoping for some suburban cop to pull me over so I could tell him all about my new friends from Ladallia. He'd maybe allow me to sleep it off in a quiet cell for about a week. I reached over and twisted the knob on the radio. "Rocket Man" by Elton John came on full blast.

Sure, space aliens. I'm nuts now. I slept with a crazy girl and I was the first to discover that mental illness is passed by sexual contact so now I'm crazy, too. I had seen things I couldn't explain and I'd better not tell. I probably should make up a pretty good alternate story so I wouldn't spend the remainder of my diminishing youth in the Buffalo Psychiatric Center.

Just under the level of the music, I heard her cry. I turned off the radio. Her thin shoulders shook. She hunched over and held her fists up to her cheeks. She stopped shaking long enough to emit the saddest little squeaks and then started shaking again.

"Alana ...."

"I'm so sorry, Sam." She pushed the words out so hard it must have hurt her throat.

I turned down a side street and parked under a tree.

"Alana ...."

"It's ... all ... my ... fault," she said, halting long enough to sob between each word.

What could I do? Next to me was this beautiful, fragile thing who was losing control and begging for my forgiveness. She could have been reciting the dictionary and I still would have wrapped my arm around her shoulders, put my hand against the side of her head, and stroked her golden hair. She went on about having found some information that could save her king, having to run away, hide until a friend could come for her, which will save the empire, but the bad guys followed her to Earth to kill her, and she was trying to do the right thing. But it was no use because soon she'd be dead which she deserved for being such a stupid girl and now she'd brought me into it, too. I was wonderful, brave, and kind, and she was so lucky to have found me, but I was unlucky, because this couldn't end good for me either, all because of her. And she was so, so sorry.

Of course, none of what she said made any sense. Still, I enjoyed holding her and even enjoyed the wet spot on my shirt from her tears and her runny nose. And a small part of me said, why not? Bodies don't explode and skinny white guys should feel pain and can't whip me, let alone Big Daddy. This made as much sense as any other crazy explanation I could come up with, and, besides, I got to hold a girl who looked a lot like Farrah Fawcett.

"Why don't they just show up with a big spaceship and blow everything up?"

"Come on, Sam. That doesn't make any sense."

"You're right. I'm just talking crazy."

"I mean, Ladallia is way too far from Earth for regular space travel. And our worlds are so different. Atmosphere, density, pressure tolerance. The only way we can come here is to be seeded and take human form."

"So ... this isn't your real form?"

"It's real," she said, looking up at me all puppy-eyed.

"But you look different on Ladallia."

She nodded.

"What do you look like, I mean, back where you live?"

"You already saw me, Sam."

"I did?"

"At the fire."

I took my fingers and ran them over the side of her face, whirled them over her neck. A haunted feeling crept through me, somewhere between a bad memory and a pleasant dream. "Why—" I didn't even know how to finish the question.

"This?" She waved at her face. "Some of it is me. I never transferred before so I'm not really good at it, but I think I left an imprint of my own when I was seeded. But the rest? You were so helpless when you lay on your back at the fire. It wasn't right for you to die after you had been so brave. I looked inside you and copied what you found pleasing."

I didn't know if I should jump out of the car and run away screaming or hug her and give her the deepest kiss I could manage.

"I think you're wonderful, Sam. You deserve to be happy."

I chose the latter, bending down and softly touching my lips to hers, making sure I registered every sensation of texture and pore. I wrapped my arms around her. I realized that in spite of almost being killed and facing worse tomorrow, I was probably the luckiest guy in the entire world, because if she wasn't an actual angel, she was the closest to it any man could ever find.

She broke away and spoke into my neck. "But, Sam, you mustn't let anything scare me. That's how they can find me."

I nodded and ran my fingers over her lips. "How long will you be here?"

"Someone's coming for me. Then I will be safe."

"When?"

She threw her arms around my shoulders and held me tight. "I hope he never comes."

***

Rich cared more about his broken shotgun than the fact that he'd lost his first fight since the second grade. I ran to the car, took five hundred dollars out the suitcase, and waved it under his nose. That brought a smile back to his face. Then I told him a lie about the two guys running away and that it would be better if I found another place for Alana.

I drove through the East Side to the sound of Smokey Robinson's "Cruisin'" on my radio, with my best girl from outer space tucked under my arm. From a few blocks down, I pointed out the tall spire. Where the ghetto met Main Street, on a triangular lot, we came to the Gothic building of dark stone. Made visible by the streetlight on the corner, there stood the crooked sign in need of repainting: The Church of the New Jerusalem, Pastor Donald Carver Presiding. I got out to unlock the gate and tucked the Crown Vic into the garage. With my firefighting lantern, I led her through the front door and down the aisle between the pews. The stained-glass windows brought a little bit of pale color to the pews and tile floor.

"It's so dark," she said, squeezing my hand.

"Electricity's off in here. Come with me." The beam from my flashlight bobbed over the altar.

She stopped in front of the crucifix. "We have that symbol on Ladallia. What does it mean here?"

I shined my light over the crude cross that might have stretched eight feet from side to side.

"It helps us to remember that Jesus died for us."

"Jesus?"

"The Son of God."

"How does a god's son die?"

"He was crucified. Nailed to a cross of wood. He sacrificed his life for us."

Alana pulled her arms around herself. "Why did God let his own son suffer?"

"He suffered to take away the guilt of our sins."

"Jesus must have been very brave."

"Yes, he was. And he loved us all very much."

She walked up two steps and stopped directly under the cross. She took her hands and held them in front of her face, then stretched them out sideways. "Feet, too?"

"Yes."

She set one foot on top of the other and rested her head on her shoulder. Her hands hung loosely at the end of her wrists. "How long did it take?"

"Alana ...." I stepped towards her.

"It must have taken a long time for him to die."

I ran to her and rested my hand on her shoulder. She whirled to face me, biting her lip, her eyes misty. "I'm going to have to be very brave, aren't I?"

My heart thumped hard against my ribs. I grabbed her by the shoulders and felt like I should pick her straight up and raise her over my head like I did to Rae. No one was going to hurt her. I'd die first. "Don't talk like that. I'll protect you. Until your friend comes for you. You're going to be safe."

She ran her fingers over my cheek. "My brave hero."

I pulled her by the hand, and she followed me down into the pastor's office. The warped door yielded with a little push. I walked over to the end table next to the couch and flicked on the crooked lamp that was missing its shade. The walls were dark wood all the way up to the ceiling. A rolltop desk stacked with old papers sat neglected in the corner. A plastic Christmas tree leaned against the opposite wall next to stacked boxes marked Holiday Decorations in black marker. Next to that was a tall wardrobe with whirls and flowers carved on the door.

"Dad comes here maybe once a month, putters a bit and sweeps up. Sometimes I stop by to check on the place, make sure there's no food around, nothing to interest the rats."

"There's rats?"

"Alana, we're in the city. But they don't hang out where they can't eat."

I yanked on the bottom of the couch and it became a double bed. I pulled off the sheets and pillowcases and shook them to check for any stray critters. "I think we're good," I said. I turned on the small space heater in the corner. "It won't do for a winter's day, but it's still at least forty degrees out."

She stood by the bed and quickly shed her clothes, then twisted her head so that her hair flared out like gold thread. The red light from the space heater gave her skin a rose hue. She looked like a goddess.

She caught me staring. "Did I do something wrong?"

"You do that so easily. Clothes on, clothes off. Like it doesn't matter."

She held her hands at her waist. "Don't you want to lay with me?"

I might have torn every button off my shirt and ripped the elastic on my jockey shorts, but in short order we were both naked and under the covers, face to face. She breathed deeply, closed her eyes. "I've been a lot of trouble, haven't I?"

"I'm used to trouble."

I studied her face, the curve of her eyelids, the slope of her cheeks. "How long 'til they rescue you?"

"I'm not sure. Finding somebody a galaxy away isn't easy. I'll know when they're close."

"What's it like? Ladallia, I mean."

"Different. The sun is pink. On Earth, the basic colors are brown and green. Oh, how I love the luscious greens you have. On Ladallia, there's lots of yellows and blues. Some purple."

"What are the people like?"

She shrugged. "Not much different than here. Most are good. Some aren't."

"And the people who are chasing you?"

"Those are the bad ones."

"But your bodies, are they like fire?"

"Not really fire. The words you use to describe it don't match ours. It's like—" She looked up for a minute to think. "Energy. Like electricity, maybe. But it's not the same."

"How do you ...?" I ran my fingertips across her shoulder.

"How do we touch? We do, but like I said, it's not the same. Your hand would go right through me."

I stroked her arm. "I think I'd like to go into you. You know, not just my junk, but to be so close to the real you."

She leaned in and pecked my lips then ran her tongue over her teeth. "I kind of like it better like this. Tastes and smells. All your nerve endings are on the outside, like you're just dying to make contact."

"Isn't everybody trying to do that?"

She ran her fingertips up and down my chest and stomach. "You people. You're so funny."

"You people?"

"You Earth people. Are all Black people this sensitive? Earth people are funny. You try so hard. But with your skin to protect you and your thoughts stuck in your head, you just can't reach out like we can, like you'd like to do."

"So that's bad."

"Maybe. I don't know. Maybe it's not bad. Maybe your god wants to see you try to overcome all the barriers he set before you. I can see why you get into so much trouble, how you fight with each other, and how you fail to see the obvious."

"Like what?"

"Like when somebody loves you. Cindy and Rae for instance."

"Cindy thinks ... well, me and her, she thinks it was a big mistake."

"Maybe. But she still loves you."

"She said that?"

"Not in words. Maybe in the way she says your name. Even the way she criticizes you. You share with her something that will keep you together always: beautiful little Rae."

"You're not going to nag me, too, are you?"

"No, Sam. I said I think you're wonderful and I promised you I'll never lie to you. You do some of the worst things, and then it makes me so proud of you when you try to do the right ones. You are a good man, Sam Carver. I couldn't have chosen anyone better."

We spent the night trying to keep warm in a musty bed. Off to the side was a closet-sized bathroom with a toilet that barely worked and a sink that spit out brown water for thirty seconds before you could drink it.

I hadn't been so happy in a long time.

***

I tried to ignore the morning sounds of horns, tires on pavement, and the hissing of the air brakes on the trucks. I heard her soft breath and watched her slender torso slowly rise and fall.

I nuzzled my nose into the back of her head.

"Hungry, darling?" I asked.

"Ummm. Food. Good idea."

"How about if I run out and get something?" I asked. "I hate to have you walking around after last night."

She turned to me, her hair tangled in front of her eyes. She smacked her lips. "I don't really want to be left alone."

"I think it'll be best if I kept you inside."

"With the rats and all those noises?"

"I think you're safer if you stay," I said.

She slithered over and, before I knew it, she was lying on my chest, our noses were touching, and she was speaking into my mouth.

"I think I'm safest with you," she said and kissed me.

"We're going to have to get food eventually."

She kissed me again, longer this time. "Maybe I'm not hungry anymore."

I grabbed two handfuls of her hair and kissed back hard. Our lips smacked when we broke apart.

"There's this little place by Lake Erie," I said. "They have all day breakfast specials."

"Gives us plenty of time."

Loud cusses came from the church floor. Alana jumped off me and brought the covers up to her nose. I swung my legs over the side of the bed. The springs creaked. I pulled my shorts up and slipped into my shoes, then crept to the door and put my ear to it. I heard steps on the creaky floorboards. I looked back to see only Alana's eyes and the top of her head. I could see her shiver right through the blanket.

Slowly, I pulled on the knob, trying to overcome the warped floor with a minimum of noise. With a pow, the door pushed toward me. I darted back to avoid getting clanked in the head. There stood my father, his head bent, his eyes dark with concentration, his three-fifty-seven shaking as he pointed it forward.

"Sam," he said. "Son of a bitch. What you doing in here, son? Where in hell are your clothes?" He shuffled in and craned his neck so that he could see around me. "Now, who the hell is that? You're not using the house of the Lord as a den of fornication, are you?"

"Dad, you scared the shit out of me."

"Well, you shouldn't be here no how. What's this?" He stepped closer to the bed and gestured with his gun hand. "You better come out of there right away, young missy."

Alana slowly drew the covers down, exposing her body. I waved back to her. "Just stay there. And keep covered."

"Well, well, well," Dad said. "A little white meat. Can't say that I don't understand the attraction." He smacked his lips. "Come on out of there right now, you sweet thing. I don't bite."

"Dad, no! Alana, stay right where you are." I stepped to one side and guided his gun so that if pointed toward the floor, then took it from him. I flipped the safety and tucked it in his pocket.

He stretched up to his full height, jabbed his finger skyward, and spoke in a strong voice. "Ye who lies with the daughters of the unclean, I shall smite down with righteous hand—"

I grabbed his arm and turned him toward the door. "Let us get dressed before you preach to us." I set my hand on his back and shut the door behind him.

"What should I do, Sam?" Alana said.

"It's just my father. Nothing to be afraid of." Although I wasn't sure. Best to keep Dad at arms' reach. And get him out of here as soon as possible.

A few minutes later, Alana followed me into the main part of the church. My dad sat in the front pew. "Dad ...."

"Now, you listen to me, Sam Carver. I may be old, but I still got my wits about me. It's clear to me now why you've been so keen to turn all my earthly belongings over to you."

"You don't understand—"

He cut me off. "Oh, I understand just fine. You intend to turn the house of the Lord into a pit of fornicators, drug users, and other ungodly creatures."

"That's not it—"

"I haven't forgotten how you ended up in rehab. My own flesh and blood stooping so low as to stick a needle in his arm. You ruined your marriage to that lovely girl and left my granddaughter without a father. Maybe some others would have cast you out but because of my Christian nature ...."

"Christian nature?" I shouted.

"Don't you raise your voice in a holy place."

I spread my arms out over my head and turned around. "There haven't been people in these pews for years."

"You know how it was when I started getting older, and then your mother died ...."

"Come on. You started losing your members long before that."

"Times change, with all these do-what-you-want-to congregations spreading their immorality."

"It wasn't the modern churches. People started to see through you, Dad."

"Honor thy Father and Mother and keep holy the house of the Lord. Don't disgrace it by bringing in harlots."

I stepped back and pulled Alana forward. "She has a name. Alana. And she's no harlot."

"You intend to marry this girl?"

I looked back at her. "I'm not sure if that would work out."

"Harlot."

"Son of a bitch." I had to force myself not to yank him up by the collar. My hands shook. "How could you, after how you treated my mother."

His eyes darted back and forth over my face. "It's true your mother and I had our rough periods, but we learned to work things out."

"Work things out? You humiliated her. You destroyed your reputation and made her look like a fool."

"Sam," Alana said softly. I felt her hand on my shoulder.

"You know what, Dad? If I were you, I'd burn this place down. How can you even drive by it after what you did?"

A bark boomed from outside. Dad turned his head and shouted. "Shut up, Chester."

"Did you ever think of me, Dad?"

He pushed himself to a standing position, his nose pointed upward defiantly. "I made my peace a long time ago. I confessed to Jesus Christ and I tried to set things right with your mom. I thought I'd raised a man. You didn't have to work like I did, you so tall and handsome and with words sliding off your tongue, spending your youth throwing a ball up and down a football field. I spent mine with the sun on my back working the fields of my daddy's farm. You had every chance. More than I ever did. If your life isn't righteous, don't look at me. There's a big mirror in that room that you were using to bone this white meat here."

I screamed and raised my hand. He jutted out his chin.

Alana's arms were on my chest, stroking me. "No, Sam."

"Well, then, seems like this little white girl here got more sense than you do," Dad said.

Another bark echoed through the empty church. I saw a brown blur flip through the spaces between the pews and heard the clatter of sharp claws and the rasp of metal dragged over the wooden floor. A pit bull slid and slammed into the front stairs of the altar, dragging a long chain, working his frying pan-sized paws to get a grip. He turned and ran our way. His head was the size of a whole ham, his shoulders rippled with muscles; his bark came from deep in his chest, ripping through the quiet church air.

Alana screamed and hid behind me. I felt her hands trembling on my waist. I backed up, spreading my arms to protect her.

The dog leaped so that his jaws were at throat level. I put my hands on his shoulders and pushed him back. He landed on his haunches, scrambled for a foothold, and jumped again. I slid my hand under his collar. His head tilted sideways, and he tried to gnaw on my wrist. I flung him backwards. He spun and coiled his back legs for another try.

Womp. My dad slapped him on the head. Chester shook his jowls and snorted. "Bad dog," Dad yelled and smacked him again. Chester looked confused and snorted some more. Dad grabbed his collar and looked up at me and Alana. I hadn't seen that sneer in years. "Thought I tied him up real good on the railing. The man I got him from said he's a good ratter. Rough and tumble, just what I need. Thing is, he said he doesn't care much for white people, neither. He'll tear them apart given half a chance." He shuffled past the altar, yanking Chester along, passing by the cross of Our Lord, and headed down the center aisle. "I trust that you and this pretty little white girl are done with your business. Make sure you lock up before you leave."

In God's house, I felt the devil in my heart. My body tensed up and I stepped forward. Alana wrapped her arms around me. "Let him go, Sam."

"After all, this is still my church," he called back in a rough voice.

"And that ain't fixin' to change any time soon."

The door slammed. I slumped onto the bench. Alana wrapped her arms around me and set her head against my chest. After a few moments of mumbling to myself, I realized that Alana was shivering.

I'd been so selfish. My father and the dog must have scared the shit out of her. "Don't pay any attention to him," I said. "You're not a harlot. You're an angel." I held her face between my hands. Her teeth chattered. She looked pale. "Baby, don't let him bother you. He's an angry old man."

She nodded weakly. "I know. He's your father. But the dog ...."

"Don't worry. My dad took him home. If he ever comes near you again, I'll break his fucking neck."

"He scared me, Sam."

"It's okay now."

"No, Sam. You don't understand. That's how they can find me."

We sat next to each other for a few minutes, Alana leaning against me. I looked up at the cross. A bitter taste crept up my throat. What kind of church was this?

"I'll take you away," I said. "We'll jump in the car and drive all day. Maybe go to my cousin's house in the suburbs. Or, hell, we'll head out west and sleep in the car."

"I can't," she said. "The one that's trying to save me, he won't find me if I run. I have to stay close by."

I thought of us waiting in the car by the ruts scratched into the pavement of the Central Park Plaza. Great place for the next batch of evil aliens to find us. Not to mention Fat Sal's guys.

"We can't go too far," she said.

I leaned back. We could try to hide. There were plenty of abandoned houses. There was even that high rise project that hadn't been used since the 1970s.

"How long until you think this guy is coming for you?"

"Soon."

I stood up and offered my hand. "We tried hiding. How about if we go to a place with lots of people?"

"I don't know."

"I got an idea. You said you like green, right?"

CHAPTER EIGHT

We sat on a bench that overlooked Delaware Lake. The temperature had risen to sixty, and a couple of diehards paddled around on canoes while other people took their Saturday strolls up and down the dirt paths that wove through the hills. The trees stood tall and graceful and still hung on to most of their red and gold leaves. Cone shaped evergreens poked skyward. A bicyclist in Spandex bent over his handlebars and whooshed past us. A plump woman with caramel skin and black hair that came to her waist harped in broken English to her brood of five little girls. "Keep away from the water!"

Alana sat next to me, alternately sipping hot chocolate and nibbling her jelly doughnut.

"I love food," she said. I reached over and swiped a finger-full of jelly and stuck it in my mouth. She turned to me, bowed her head, and offered me the piece that was left.

"I'm good, Alana. It's not my first doughnut like it is for you."

"Do they have any more?"

"Plenty."

I smiled, but then I looked down at the pavement. She didn't have to worry about getting fat or cavities. Because she was leaving me soon.

"Hey, Carver, how'd they let you out of the east side?"

I turned and there was a cop, around my age, olive skin. He swung his nightstick like he'd had lots of practice. It was Tony, a friend from the old days, who'd transferred from the fire department to the police.

"I don't know. I guess they'll let anybody be a cop these days." I stood up, knocked my fist into his and gave him a hug. Wearing his police cap, he came up to my chin. Curly brown hair peaked out from under it.

He shrugged. "The fire department wasn't for me. One accident too many. How's your back?"

"I get by. Just got to be a little careful."

I introduced him to Alana.

"Wow," he said. He gave Alana the once over. "I always wanted to be you, Sam."

After some more small talk, he continued his rounds, flipping his nightstick in his hand.

If anybody came after her, they'd have to do it in broad daylight with fifty people around and a cop standing by.

I watched Alana as she sipped her cocoa and licked her fingertips. Her eyes looked upward, moving from one side of the lake to the other.

"Look, Sam," she said, pointing. "The tops of the trees, they're moving." She swayed her head in time. "Like they're dancing. Then the wind kicks up, and the leaves shake."

"That's how it is in the fall," I said.

"It's wonderful."

"I'm glad you like it."

"You live in such a pretty little place."

She looked down at the sidewalk, set the cup down, knitted her brow, and held her stomach.

"Are you all right?"

Her face turned intense. Her head swiveled left and right like she heard something.

"Alana?" I grabbed her hand.

She raised a finger to quiet me before standing and facing the far side of the lake. She took one step, hesitated, then took another. Her hand slipped out of mine and she started walking down the path. Slow at first, then faster, then breaking into a trot. I rose to my feet. Down the way another figure ran toward her. He was at least my height, broad shouldered, and as fair as Alana. His golden hair fluttered over his forehead.

The cold wind pierced right through me.

I hated the feeling of saying goodbye.

Out of the depths of the park came a horrendous sound, as though someone had detonated a bomb. I could feel the aftershock on my chest. The children of the Hispanic woman ran to huddle against her skirt. She bent down and threw her arms around them. From the trees came one scream, then another. A slim elderly man with a walking stick, a pair of heavy-legged woman joggers, a quartet of young brothers carrying a basketball all ran down the hill to the pavement that bordered the lake. From the looks on their faces it was obvious they were scared shitless. They scrambled up the stairs that led to the street.

A monster jumped out of the trees and landed on the concrete, shaking its massive head so that spittle flew in all directions. Its stubby bowed legs held up a chest the size of a large garbage can. It resembled a pit bull, but couldn't be. It was closer to the size of a mastiff, or even a small horse. The shoulders and haunches bulged like they belonged on an ox. Its jaw muscles were bigger than my biceps. It turned its oversized head right, then left. Behind the slit of eyelids burned green hate. It opened its jaws into a contorted smile and exposed its six-inch incisors. Then its eyes fell on Alana and it licked its lips.

Alana turned white, buckled at the knees, and fell, catching herself on a trash can. The monster dog stepped toward her, lowering its head, and emitted a low mocking growl.

She was thirty feet from me. I ran for her. The man with the golden hair closed four times the distance in a flash, lowering his shoulder into the ribs of the dog. The creature stumbled, righted itself, and faced the man. It stretched open its jaws and roared. The man kicked at its throat; the monster snapped its jaws around his ankle.

"No!" Alana cried. She crawled forward toward the danger that would certainly kill her.

I ran faster than I had in years, the balls of my feet jabbing the concrete. I ignored the tightness in my back. She crawled two feet. I ran ten. The beast shook the man like a rag doll. Blood seeped over the its snout. The head covered with the golden hair flopped against the pavement. His arms flailed helplessly to catch hold of something.

Mothers, fathers, children, tennis players, and maintenance workers, the park emptied as they scattered in all directions.

Alana, who'd cringed at the normal-sized dog in the church, scrambled forward, stretched out, and slapped the monster on the face. It stopped, bent its head and spit out the leg, then stretched open its mouth. The killer teeth dripped with dark red.

I dove for her, snatching Alana by the hood of her sweatshirt and pulling her just out of the reach of the snap of those massive jaws. The beast reared up to snap again. I darted in front of her; it'd have to go through me first.

The man with the golden hair dove in and wrapped his arms around the monster's neck. His bloody leg dangled behind him, deep red spurting out. With his good leg, he pushed up and tried to mount the creature's back. He shouted at me, "Get her out of here."

The dog thing stretched its head upward, then twisted, and fell on its back and scraped against the sidewalk. The man tried to hold on, but his body left a wet red trail as the dog rubbed him into the pavement. The monster head stretched until its snout was under the neck of the golden haired man. The jaws snapped down hard. Blood gushed upward. The man fell back limply.

Alana screamed. I wrapped my arms around her and brought her to her feet.

More footsteps. I turned and there was Tony, his legs apart enough to make a firm base, his shoulders squared, his arms thrust forward and meeting at the handle of his nine millimeter.

"Get the fuck out of here, Sam," he said. "I got backup coming."

The golden-haired man was a mess of twisted limbs and blood. A thread of skin kept his head connected to his torso. Alana struggled to stand. I pulled her back.

"We've got to go," I cried next to her ear.

"I can't leave him."

"He's already dead."

There was a flash of light and the body was gone. Tony stood up and dropped his gun to his side. His face hung.

The dog lunged. Tony righted himself quickly, fired once, twice. Blood and fur ripped off the dark brown hide. The monster raised its head and howled.

"Run!" Tony called. He kept the gun trained while he backed up.

I yanked on Alana's arm and ran. We'd made it to the bottom of the stairs when I heard two shots followed by a yelp. We'd gotten halfway up when more shots came, two, three more and then a snarl. I took the last step up to the street, turned, and snatched Alana up to me. If I bent just right, I could see the battle still going on. I watched Tony's gun rapidly spit flame. The monster hesitated, then dove forward and pushed Tony to the ground. Tony brought his hands up, pulled the trigger. All that came out were empty clicks. The creature grunted; it sounded like a laugh. The jaws opened and snapped into arms, hands, and head. My old friend laid still. The monster took a second to savor the flesh in its mouth before it turned to face us. Its eyes were full of sulfuric hate and its shoulders were streaked with blood where bullets had torn into its hide.

I screamed to Alana, "Run for the car and lock the door."

My car was parked across the street in front of the art gallery. The building of white marbles and pillars looked like it came right out of old Rome. People scrambled up the dozens of steps against a backdrop of screams and car horns playing an ugly soundtrack.

I took the lead and guided her through the mess of people, knocking aside a young couple who ran in front of us. I held Alana's arm firmly, stopping her right before a car shot by. When there was an opening in traffic, I led her across the street, pushed her into the Crown Vic, and slid into the front seat.

I slammed my door. "Get down Alana," I shouted, hoping we'd lost the thing in the crowd. No such luck. I heard a wild roar and saw it standing directly across the street, licking the blood off its lips, scanning left and right until its green eyes settled on me.

My hand shook as I turned the key and pumped the gas. The motor sputtered. I wished I'd gotten that tune up. "Come on, damn you."

The Godzilla of pit bulls romped toward me. A car slammed on its brakes and skidded out of the way. The dog pulled back, seeming to study the traffic before it leaped forward.

The motor coughed out a metallic howl. I threw it in gear and hit the gas. Four hundred horses caught and heaved the car into the street. The tires spun. I smelled the burning rubber. It seemed like forever, but in a flash we got traction and shot down the parkway.

I looked over at Alana. She stared ahead. Her face was white.

"It's okay," I said. "You're going to be safe now."

She shook her head slowly. "More death."

"It's not your fault."

"I didn't think this would happen. I tried to do the right thing."

I slowed down at the stop sign just enough to look both ways, then gunned it through the intersection.

I was going sixty on a street posted at thirty. On either side were three- and four-story mansions of brown and red stone. They had turrets and back houses for the hired help, with massive lawns and long driveways. Don't worry. white people. At this rate, I'll be out of your neighborhood in a few seconds.

I heard the crunch of metal and felt the car jerk to the side. I crossed the yellow line and a pickup truck swerved to avoid me. Tires screeched. I fought to right the steering wheel. Alana screamed.

Her window shattered. She cowered next to me, covering her head with her hands, and falling into my lap. Glass rained down and the sharp crystals bit my face. Monster-dog was next to us, keeping pace at sixty, snorting with every breath, its head and shoulders bobbing up and down with each stride. It swung its massive skull into the side of the door. The car jerked and ran up on the sidewalk.

A few yards ahead, two young girls jogged, their hair in ponytails, wearing identical green and white sweats from the local private school. My car tobogganed at them. They grabbed each other and stiffened.

If I didn't do something, I would add two more to the body count.

I twirled the steering wheel frantically. The rear end of the Crown Vic tore up the lawn and fishtailed to the left. I slammed on the gas and shot us into the street. With a thud, the right corner panel hit the creature. It rolled over several times before righting itself.

I tore forwards, straddling the double yellow line. The monster galloped next to Alana's side, stuck its head through the window, and snapped. Alana screamed and crammed as close to me as possible.

We rushed through another intersection. Cars slammed on their brakes and hit their horns. Houses and parked cars zipped by. The monster pushed in, its sharp black claws reaching through the window fighting to catch hold, its hungry mouth snapping and inching closer.

I went right and swiped the sides of the parked cars hoping to compress Man's Best Freak into a giant doggie burger. Its head rattled against the roof and it fell.

I hit the brakes. The car skidded to a halt. I looked out my rearview mirror. The monster laid flat and motionless. I sighed. Then it twitched, brought its stout legs under it, stood, and shook its over-sized head.

Oh, no, you don't.

I threw the car in reverse. The engine screamed. The transmission whined. "Hang on," I told Alana.

There was a clunk. I remembered the horror movies where the guy neglects to finish off the monster when it's down, so the monster comes back and eats him. I drove the car forward a few feet, then revved it in reverse. The shock absorbers almost came through the floor; it felt like I had run over a side of beef.

I jumped out, slammed the door, hurried around the rear, and peeked down the passenger's side. Fido with the overactive thyroid laid under the car just ahead of the back wheel. Its paws stuck out at right angles from its body.

I stood over that mass of muscle and torn skin and bad intentions and watched it set its paws under its chest and push up. Metal creaked and the car rose a foot. The beast shimmied forward and fell again. It laid flat as if to gather its strength, then pushed a second time. At the rate it was going, it'd be free in a few moments.

I ran to the back, opened the trunk, and pulled out the pick axe I'd borrowed from the firehouse. "Here, little doggy, I got something for you," I taunted.

I stood over it and brought the axe to my shoulder. The skin was rubbed away on one side of its face. It closed its eyes, grunted, and pushed again. The car jumped up and down. Its hind legs were almost free.

"Let's see if you explode real nice like your buddies."

After four solid whacks, its head opened like a melon. I stepped back. It made an impressive sparkly poof on its way to hell.

***

Apparently a 1980 Ford is harder to kill than a creature from the alien dog pound. In spite of a smashed door, a broken side window, and a shimmy in the front end, I sped away ahead of the approaching wail of police sirens. I didn't have a good explanation for what had happened and, for Alana's sake, I couldn't spend the next twenty-four hours in police custody trying to make up a story the cops would swallow.

I passed Main Street and returned to the 'hood, where at least I gained the illusion of safety.

"You okay?"

Eyes closed, Alana leaned her head back on the seat and nodded.

I had a job where I risked my life every day, so I was hard to rattle.

But I was rattled now. "Listen, you've got to help me here," I said,

Her voice shook. "I want you to know, I was trying to do good. For my world. I thought if there was any danger, it would be for me. I didn't know I was bringing all this trouble to others."

"I know the feeling."

"I am so sorry about your friend."

Something stiffened inside of me. Poor Tony.

"Alana, tell me. Why did they send a dog? I mean, he was an impressive dog, but ...."

"Ladallia and Earth are far apart, Sam. Since our bodies are energy, we can be shot over the galaxy. But it's not completely accurate. They can't follow me by sight. But when I'm afraid, it's like a beacon."

"So when you were scared by a pit bull in the church ...."

"They got an impression of what I was afraid of and sent that." She stopped and turned toward the window.

"That guy with the hair like you?"

"He came to rescue me."

"He was a brave man."

She nodded and squished up her face like she was about to cry.

"Will your people send someone else?"

"They'll try. With the information I have, I'm very important to both sides."

"Okay. So we just need to find you a safe place where you won't be afraid." She'd be comfortable with Cindy and Rae, but I couldn't put my ex and my daughter at risk. If I dropped Alana off at Willie's, he might go off on a rant and I'd have to contend with a ten-foot Willie next time. I'd rather face the monster dog again. My father had the pit bull now, so I couldn't leave her at his house or even at church.

I thought of something. "You're not afraid of wood, are you?"

***

In the 1930s, there was a car manufacturer called Pierce Arrow. The complex sprawled over hundreds of acres on the west side of Buffalo. By the 1980s, the car company was long gone but the structures still stood. Now it was a maze of four-, five-, and six-story buildings broken up into hundreds of small manufacturers, cabinet makers, upholsters, and home improvement concerns.

First stop was the firehouse. Lucky that Joe wasn't one to hold a grudge. He had a small wood shop at the warehouse for his side business as a carpenter. I promised to work for him the next two weekends if I could use his shop for a couple of days. But first I had to listen to the story.

"Did you hear, Sam? A cop was killed at Delaware Park. Everybody's talking about it."

"That's too bad." Really bad for my old friend Tony.

"People said it was a dog. And not just any dog, but a six-foot killer with steak knives for teeth. Can you believe that? The chief said everybody should grab an axe when they get off the rig."

"If I see a dog like that, I'm going to run his ass over," I said.

Finally, he gave me the keys to his warehouse. While pulling away, I spied the big black limo that belonged to Fat Sal's boys, coming up fast from the rear. But the Crown Vic still had some guts, and I knew this neighborhood a hell of a lot better than they did. I weaved in and out of streets with a smile on my face so I didn't let on to Alana, so she wouldn't be scared. In a minute, we were free and clear and we cruised out of the 'hood.

At the Pierce Arrow complex, the Crown Vic sputtered as I navigated the canyon of vertical walls and right angles. After several turns, I parked and led her up the stairs and through the stone hall.

"See? Nothing to be afraid of," I said, slapping the recently painted cinderblock walls. My voice echoed down the long well-lit corridor. We passed a few doors with business names stenciled on translucent glass until I came to Joe's Woodworking. I turned the key and ushered her in. The front room was a neat, small office. A TV hung from the ceiling. She walked around, flipped through the girlie calendar on the wall, looked out the window, and, with her finger, tweaked the dangling leaves from the hanging plant.

"You can sit there." I pointed to the chair behind the desk. "And you use this to change the channels." I showed her how to use it, then I made her a hot chocolate on the hot plate that sat on the small table in the corner. Joe had even left a Snicker's bar in his desk.

"What's behind the door?"

I wanted to make sure there was nothing around that would scare her. I motioned to her. I clicked the lock open, and we peeked in. "This is the stuff Joe uses to make things. That's a table saw and that's a lathe. You can make all kinds of pretty things out of wood." Joe kept the shop as neat as his office. Tools hung up on peg board, coffee cans with screws, nails, and bolts lining the back of a tall sturdy table. Wood was stacked neatly in the corner. "It's a nice place," I said. "Nothing to be afraid of."

She nodded and continued to walk around, arms wrapped around herself, shoulders slouched.

"It's just for a little while," I said.

"I don't want you to go," she said, kicking at the floor.

"I have to do some things so that you're safe until they come to rescue you."

She fell against me and hung on tight. She was so frail. I ran my hand over her spine and felt her slight ribs, the firm rise of her butt. I put my nose against her hair. She had her own special odor, like some tropical flower.

"Come on, let me go do my man thing so I can keep you safe." I took her by the arm and led her to the chair. I reached down and grabbed her ankles and propped her feet on the desk. "There. You'd make a good firefighter." I handed her the Snicker's. She studied it, sniffed, then tentatively bit into the wrapper. She held it at arms' length and wrinkled her nose.

"I don't like it."

I took it from her and undid the top of the wrapper. She nibbled. A smile came to her face.

"I'll be back soon," I said.

"Bye, Sam," she said and held up the candy bar. "Oh, and bring back some more of these."

***

So I was still playing life like a crazy juggler who had too many balls in the air. Except God had just dropped a couple of bowling balls at my head simply to fuck with me. I had to keep Alana safe and from being afraid. We'd hang out at Joe's office. It was the weekend, and the building should be quiet. Keep things light, have some fun, watch TV, and sleep on the blankets I had in the trunk, order take out. Soon her people would arrive on the extra-terrestrial express and I'd be back to my regular life.

I thought of Alana's sweet face. Cindy's words knocked around inside my head: to do the right thing. I had to concentrate on stuff like that because the last thing I wanted to dwell on was how empty I felt before I met Alana. And, as sure as there was smog over the Buffalo skyline, I knew I was bound to lose her soon.

Poor Tony. Poor Mona. I was going to make sure there would be no more deaths, unless it was some alien motherfuckers.

I wasn't going to be taken by surprise again. I needed some firepower to protect her. That brought me to Willie's house. He kept his own mini arsenal. Tough as nails, every gangbanger in the city still looked up to him. If he couldn't give me something, he'd know where to send me.

After squeezing into a parking space, I walked up the wooden stairs onto the creaky porch and knocked. I looked around. Each two-story house had a postage stamp lawn. Tree trunks stretched straight and tall like pillars, limbs full of green and hints of gold vaulting over the street. Narrow driveways separated the houses. The sun settled down behind the trees and slithered through the autumn air. There were lots of reasons not to like the 'hood, but at times like this, it felt like home.

The metal screen door croaked when Willie threw it open. "What the fuck are you doing here?" he said. "We got to go to work in an hour."

"I called in sick."

"Motherfucking Turk. You do look like shit." He craned his neck out the door. "What the fuck did you do to your car?"

"You know how I kid you about your being really, really dark? Now that I see you in the sunlight, it doesn't help at all. You're still black as pitch."

"Did you come here to talk about my complexion?"

"I need your help, Willie."

"Uh-oh. I got seventy bucks in my jacket. It's all yours."

"Can I come in?"

I sprawled on his couch. He handed me a can of beer and sat on the chair across from me. We popped tabs and sipped. "Just tell me what you need," he said.

"I need a gun."

"Whoa, cousin. Slow down. That's serious shit."

"I *am* serious, Willie. Can you help me?"

"I ain't sure this is a good idea."

"Please."

"Is this for the Italians? Don't do it. You're never gonna win that kind of fight with them. If you get one or two, they'll still come back. Maybe even involve your family."

With all the worrying I was doing about Alana, I'd forgotten to take care of Fat Sal's guys. "That's not it."

"You gotta start paying them. Either that or leave town."

Damn. I didn't come here to get lectured. "It's not the Italians. I got that all wrapped up."

"Don't bullshit a bullshitter."

"I swear it isn't them."

"Is it the girl?"

I took a deep breath to try to calm myself because I was getting really pissed off. "Why do you say that?"

"Listen, Sam. Something ain't right with that chick."

"Let's not go there."

"I'm serious, cous. You ain't been the same since she showed up."

"Don't lecture me."

"It's like she took away your edge. It used to be you giving it to the bitches, even if it got you in trouble. Now it's like she's the one standing over you and all you can see is what's between those long creamy legs."

Hot blood flushed through my face. "Why can't you just help me with what I came here for?"

"You're whipped, Sam. Pussy whipped. This little cunt has got you all wrapped up—"

I stood up and clenched my fists, crushing the beer can. Foam squirted out over the rug. "Shut the fuck up. Don't you ever call her a cunt. You don't know what you're talking about. What do you know about women? You're almost fifty, and you're stuck in this crappy little apartment, sitting all alone in the dark, drinking your liver into oblivion."

He slowly rose to his feet. "Who the fuck do you think you're talking to?"

"Don't you ever call her that, old man. I will fuck you up. I will—"

He stopped me by slapping me hard. I rubbed the sting on my cheek. Willie gave me a stare that could stop a madman cold.

"See what I just did, Sam? I'm gonna lay this out for you. You ain't tough. Not street tough, at least. Sure, you're a great firefighter. There's nobody I'd rather have watching my back at a fire than you and I love you for it. But you spent all those years throwing a football around, being treated like a star. You know what I was doing when I was a teenager? I was fighting. Every day. So don't get so full of yourself." He turned and walked into the back room.

I felt pretty humble, because he was right. When I first came to Engine 39, straight out of rehab, Willie took me under his wing, showed me everything he knew. If I was anything as a firefighter, I owed it to him. If we were in a tough spot in a fire, I knew it was going to be all right if he was next to me.

He came back out and pulled a pistol from his pocket. "You ever fired a handgun?"

"Once or twice."

"This is a thirty-eight revolver that somebody threw in the fields. It's a little beaten up, but I've tested it." He showed me how to load it, how to use the safety, how to aim, and shoot. I reached for it. He pulled it behind his back. "Now, don't be stupid. If you shoot someone with an unregistered gun, you're going to lose your job and go to jail. So if push comes to shove and you got to use it, you get rid of it. Okay?"

I nodded. He handed me the gun and a box of shells.

"You use a forty-four," I said. "I mean, will this put someone down with one shot?"

He patted the box of shells. "Hollow points. It'll put down anything this side of a moose."

"Thanks."

"You want me to come with you?"

There was nothing I wanted more than to have Willie back me up, but I couldn't bring him into this. Not after what had happened to Tony and Mona.

"I got to do this myself."

"Fucking hardhead," he said. He grabbed my shoulders, pulled me against his chest, and kissed me on the cheek. When he stepped away, I saw that his eyes were moist. "You take care of yourself. You hear me? I love you, Sam."

I stepped toward the door and looked back at the slump-shouldered man in the sad dark room. "You're a good friend," I said.

"Friends for life, Sam."

The phone rang. Willie bent down to the end table and picked up the receiver. "Yeah? Hold it, Joe. Slow the fuck down."

"Joe from the firehouse?" I said. Willie waved me away with his hand. I ran up to him and snatched the phone.

"Joe, it's Sam. Is everything all right?"

"Sam, I'm so sorry. I didn't mean to let you down. They scared the shit out of me. I had to tell them."

"Joe, calm down and tell me what happened."

"I was sitting on the bench when these three guys came by in a black limo. Fuck, they were so big. They said they knew who I was and where my family stayed. I'm sorry, Sam. I panicked."

"Joe, what did you do?"

"I told them where you were. Or where I thought you were. I called the office after they left to let you know, but nobody answered. Thank God you're safe. I'd never forgive myself."

No, they wouldn't find me, but they *would* find Alana. I could call the office to warn her, but she didn't even know what a telephone was. I slammed down the receiver and ran for the door.

"Hold up, cous," Willie called.

"I gotta go, Willie."

CHAPTER NINE

I raced back to the warehouse while my mind worked over the possibilities, all of them bad. The money I needed to pay the Italians had been sitting in my trunk. I was so worried about protecting Alana that I wasn't paying attention. If they hurt her … but they wouldn't. That wasn't good for business. Maybe they'd leave her with a little scare. Maybe they were waiting at Joe's office and I could pay them and get them out of my hair.

I ran up the stairs and through the corridors, screaming her name. The answer came back in my own hollow echo. I turned the corner to the long hallway that led to Joe's office. Her haunting whimper wended its way off the stone and concrete and into my ears. I burst inside the office. She sat on the floor in the corner, her arms around her knees, her head down and covered with the green hood.

I dove in front of her, held my hands next to her body, afraid to touch her, afraid to find that she'd suffered something awful. She looked up and the only thing wrong with her face was her eyes red from crying. Her lips trembled. She reached out for me and I wrapped my arms around her.

I stroked the back of her head. "You're not hurt, are you?"

She pushed away, shook her head, and wiped her nose with her sleeve.

I helped her up and led her back to the chair. I sat on the edge of the desk. "Tell me what happened."

"They were awful. At first, I thought they had come from my planet but then they didn't try to kill me. They started talking quietly and said they were my friends, but I didn't believe them. One of them opens the door," she gestured to the shop, "and goes in and I hear things rattling around. The others asked me where you were, and I said I didn't know. They asked when you were coming back, and I said I didn't know that, either. So the big one pulls me out of the chair and shakes me. He calls me these terrible names and his breath was terrible and his face was all sweaty.

"He said if I didn't talk, he was going to hurt me. Then he looked me up and down in this really creepy way and he said, yeah, he knew what to do with a pretty thing like me and he told me the things he was going to do and they were dirty things, Sam, and I didn't want him to touch me like that. And he said I'd like that kind of stuff, wouldn't I, and I said, no, I'd hate it. And he said that's not all because he knew how to do other stuff that would really hurt so I'd better talk.

"I started crying and I swore I didn't know where you were. And one of the other ones comes out of the room and says he's got an idea." She rested her right hand on the desk and there was a red spot like a pin prick and a tiny trail of dried blood following the crease of her palm. "So ... so, one of them holds my hand down on the desk, and the other one takes a nail and sticks it in the middle of my hand and it hurts. And the other one grabs that thing." She gestured to a hammer on the desk. "And he raises it up over his head and I thought of what they did to Jesus and I just started crying so hard and I was trying to be brave, but I'm not brave, Sam. And I'm waiting for the really painful part and one of them says, that's enough, if I knew anything I would have talked. He said did I get the message and I said yes. And he said to tell you that they would be waiting for you by the bridge near the old grocery store and you better come soon or next time ...." She slumped in the chair and covered her head.

Again the things I'd left undone were hurting those I loved. "Alana, I'm going to meet them and take care of this."

"No, Sam, they'll hurt you. They're bad men."

"They just want me to give them something. It's all right. You wait here."

"I can't wait here."

"But it will be safer here. I'll be right back."

"Don't you understand, Sam? They scared me."

***

In the 'hood, many of the side streets still looked good, where hard working people kept their houses painted and their hedges trimmed. One hundred-year-old trees arched overhead. I made a left off of the quiet residential street. My beaten-up car sputtered down the main drag through what used to be a business district but now was lined with a succession of empty lots and boarded up buildings covered in graffiti. It couldn't have looked any worse if it had been bombed. Alana sat in the back seat, a blanket pulled up to her chin. I'd made her promise that when we got to the bridge, she had to stay in the back and hide under the blanket.

I passed the street that led to the firehouse. To my right was the vacant lot with its line of abandoned cinder block box buildings. Ahead was the bridge for the railroad. The black Caddie was parked underneath. Sal's guys leaned on the side of the car like they were waiting to cause trouble.

One hundred yards away I pulled to the curb. "Okay, Alana. We're here. You bend down and cover your head, okay? This'll be over in a minute."

I wanted to ram their nice shiny limo with my Crown Vic, then jump out and start shooting. What a bunch of motherfuckers, to scare a girl like Alana.

I swallowed my anger, swung open my door, and got out. Victor became alert, stood up straight, and tugged on his dark suit. I went to the trunk, snapped open the suitcase full of money, counted out thirty-five large, and stuffed the rest into my spare tire. I slid the thirty-eight to the side of my belt to make sure it was covered by my jacket, slammed the trunk, and made my way toward them. At about fifty yards, Victor took two steps toward me and called, "I had a side bet with Leo. He said you wouldn't show. Guess he was anxious to get back to your girlfriend. Me, I said, 'Leo, you got to have faith in people.'"

"Fuck you, Victor. Does Fat Sal know you like to scare women?"

"He kinda gives us a free hand. Hey, it brought you here, didn't it? Sometimes you got to stir the pot a little. You got the money?"

I raised the briefcase. "It's here. All of it."

"So this will be a good day. You get Sal off of your back and I don't have to come looking for you anymore in this rat hole."

I stopped dead in my tracks. Victor slid his hand under his sports coat. "Now, don't get cold feet on me Sam."

I barely heard him. Because creeping up from the shadows on the underside of the bridge were three figures. They drifted down. And while they seemed to only possess one head and two arms apiece, their most notable feature was that they were composed of translucent green flame. The last time I'd seen anything like those forms was in the fire when I met Alana.

Even though the green flame was beautiful, there was a darkness in it, like hate simmering in hell.

I was struck still. I didn't feel friendly enough with Victor to stop the aliens from kicking his ass. But after Victor was gone, I knew who the three of them would go after.

"Victor, turn around. There's something behind you."

He rose up to his full height and shrugged. "You think I'm stupid or something, Sam?"

I should have run, but I was afraid Victor would draw on me and start shooting.

The green ghosties caught up to the car and hovered over the two men waiting there. These men I hated, who'd threatened me and Alana, suddenly I didn't want to see them get hurt. We were on the same team, the humans, after all, and these things, they had no faces, clearly no feelings, and maybe no souls.

The men didn't have time to scream because they were engulfed in green flame. Victor's guys writhed and fell to the pavement. Slowly, the first green form rose and its wavering flame subsided. The green turned to a light olive. Like flesh. On the heads, faces formed. A dark fog became curly brown hair. The heads looked left and right. The massive chests rose and fell. They looked at their hands, stretched out their arms.

One of the men sat up and slid backwards until he bumped into the car. Because standing over him, butt naked, was a copy of himself. Or at least a copy of what he would be if he were six inches taller and full of muscles. The cry stuck in his throat. He scrambled to pull out his pistol. Before he could point it, the naked man swatted it away, reached down, and grabbed the man's neck. The crunching sound turned my stomach.

The second man scrambled to his feet. His prayer to the Blessed Mother echoed under the bridge. His over-sized twin picked him up by the shoulders, swung him around, and slammed him into the side of the car. The two naked now-men looked at each other, then stumbled forward as they tried out their new legs.

Victor turned to the noise. He should have run, but he stood frozen and stared. The last green form hung over his head. He backed up, pulled out his pistol, got off one shot that went right through the specter and pinged off the metal bridge. Green flame engulfed him and Victor writhed. The two naked figures stepped forward and watched the sequence repeat itself. Shortly there was another naked form standing over Victor, one with Victor's rough-cut face and curly hair. The new man turned to me and bored into me with Victor's eyes, as if he knew me, with Victor's cold look, with Victor's thick brow creased in concentration. The fake Victor raised his arm and pointed at me.

"Take him," he said. "Alive. We need to find the girl." He raised his bare foot and drove it down. Victor's head, the real one, cracked like a coconut.

I wanted to puke.

The two men came at me. Their steps were awkward at first, stumbling left, then right. It was all so crazy, I couldn't move, I couldn't turn away.

Come on, Sam, if not for yourself, do it for Alana. I forced myself to backed up and I ran.

I heard their heavy bare feet slapping against the pavement, clumsy, irregular. Maybe I had time to get away. I cursed myself for not leaving the car running.

Through the windshield, from the back seat, I saw the shine of the golden hair. Alana's eyes were wild with fear.

Why the fuck didn't she stay hidden?

I made it to the car and swung open my door. The two men became more sure-footed with every step and quickly closed the distance between us. Alana screamed. The men plunged forward, one coming my way and the other to the passenger side. My knees buckled when he slapped his hands down on my shoulders. He shoved me against the door, and my back exploded in pain.

Glass broke and Alana screamed again. Out of the corner of my eye, I saw slivers of the window tinkling down on top of the blanket and his long arm reaching in for her.

The one on me was at least six and a half feet tall. His shoulders were as wide as a refrigerator. The muscles under his hairy chest rippled as he forced his gorilla hands toward my throat. I'd seen what he'd done to Sal's man, and I tried to push my arm in the way, but he worked past it like it wasn't even there. Fingers engulfed my windpipe, and a grin split his ugly mug. Suddenly I got the panicky feeling that no air was passing through my throat. I slapped his wrists with one hand and with the other reached for my gun. Instantly, I was light-headed; I struggled to pull the gun free. It was such a simple thing, but I couldn't find the trigger, wasn't sure if I were pointing it in the right direction. Without air and blood flow to my brain, I fought to concentrate. Picking up the gun was the same as raising a bowling ball. I managed to stick it under his chin. Inches away from the crack, I thought my ear drums would rupture. The life washed out of his face. I fired again. He stepped back, missing half a head, and exploded.

I allowed myself one deep breath then ran around the car. The other man yanked on Alana's hair and had her half out of the window. When I got a clean shot, I started firing, once, twice, three times into his side. He jumped and jittered, then swung at me wildly. I ducked under his arm and placed the gun against the back of his skull. The top of his head came off, then he exploded from within.

My mouth tasted like I'd licked a battery.

Then something hit my head and I saw stars. I spun in a blender stuffed with cars, trees, streetlights, and utility poles. A steel grip clamped down on my shoulders and swung me around. I thumped against the pavement. I raised my hand in front of my eyes. I barely made out the figure that had shoulders so wide that I was engulfed by the shadow. His hands curled into fists, tree trunk arms swaying at his knees. His voice was like Victor's would be if Victor's mouth were full of gravel. "You. It's always you."

Tires screeched and metal crunched against metal. Steam hissed and a car door slammed. I fought to clear my head. The fake Victor was pinned between Willie's front bumper and my rear. I felt a hand in my underarm and Willie yanked me to my feet. The monster laid over the car, still for a moment, then pushed himself up with his massive arms.

"If this don't beat all," Willie said. He pointed his forty-four under its chin. "This motherfucker could be playing defensive line for the Buffalo Bills—if he wasn't a naked wacko pervert trying to beat on my friend. You got anything to say for yourself, you stupid bastard?"

The man looked at Willie and sneered. "Kill you," he said.

"You are one confused motherfucker," Willie said.

The man lunged, his arm darting out. I pulled Willie back. The man raised one fist over his head and slammed it into the hood. Then he raised the other and did the same.

"Stop it," Willie said. "You already made me fuck up my bumper."

"Kill you."

Willie, the man who was unbelievably quick when he was at a fire, stood paralyzed. His dark face hung slack. I put one hand on his wrist and the other on his gun. He looked at me and loosened his grip. I ripped off one shot of that bad ass cannon and my target flew back and fell at an odd angle backwards over my trunk. Then came that now-familiar explosion, and he was gone.

"Son of a bitch," Willie said.

I handed the gun back to Willie and ran around to the side door. Alana sat in the middle of my back seat, her arms folded. Her hands were bloody.

"Are you all right?"

She answered in a squeaky little voice. "I think so. I just cut myself on the window."

I ran back to Willie, who hadn't moved a muscle. "We better get out of here."

"So this is how your car keeps getting fucked up." Willie said.

"Willie, there's three dead bodies under the bridge."

"What did I just see, Sam?" He stared at the spot where the man had been, where the flash occurred. His jaw hung open.

"I'll tell you later. You okay to drive?"

"Anything. Just get me the fuck out of here."

***

We rushed back to Willie's place. Willie sat on his couch, the back of his head leaning against the wall, his face two shades paler than I thought possible. Alana stood in front of me and pulled her shirt up, exposing everything up to her neck. I knelt in front of her and checked the long red marks on her stomach. "You're fine, Alana. They're little scratches, that's all."

I knew Willie was messed up because he didn't even peek at Alana's perfect little tits.

I plopped down next to Willie. Alana sat in the chair in the corner with her knees pulled up to her chin.

"Tell me again," Willie said. "Who killed the three Italians?"

"There were two other guys like the one you hit with your bumper," I said.

"He blew up," Willie said. "I saw it, didn't I? This big naked white guy was beating the mess out of you and I rammed him. You shot him." He pulled out his gun and checked the cylinder. "One bullet missing." He sniffed the barrel. "Gun's been fired. At least I'm not making that up. But this big bodybuilder motherfucker just blew up. Maybe it was the steroids. Maybe he's too high strung."

I bit my lip, stared at the ceiling.

"Maybe you want to tell me what the fuck is going on, Sam," Willie said.

I sighed. "It's complicated."

"I can try to explain it if you'd like," Alana said.

"You know what?" Abruptly Willie stood up. "I don't fucking want to know. Something crazy is going on." He pointed at Alana. "And whatever it is, it started when this little white girl showed up."

I wanted to defend Alana, but I didn't know how. I looked up at Willie. "You need to trust me on this."

"Sam, I love you like a brother. Tell me if I'm wrong, but it's her I don't trust."

"Please, Willie."

"I mean it. Look at her eyes. Look her skin. She ain't right. Look at you, Sam. You're all fucked up. You keep driving around with her in your back seat, getting into trouble."

"I'm asking you as a brother," I said. "Leave it alone, Willie."

"Whatever you say." He walked to the door and took out his car keys.

"Where are you going?"

"I'm going to work where I only got to deal with fires and car accidents and cardiac arrests. If anything blows up, there's a good reason for it. I may see some bad shit at work, but everything has an explanation. You can stay the night. I would appreciate it if, when I come here in the morning, I didn't have to look at her." He slammed the door. I heard his feet clomp down the stairs. His Caddie puttered and roared and screeched down the street.

Alana held her hands in her lap. She reminded me of a child on a construction site, bumping into things, making everybody watch after her even though they had their own work to do so that she didn't drop a circular saw on somebody's head.

"Why did you pull the blanket off your head? If you hadn't screamed, they might not have known you were there."

"They feel me, Sam. Like I can feel them."

"But, still, having a feeling is not the same as exposing yourself to them."

"I guess I got scared."

So she was afraid? What kind of people were they on Ladallia? Didn't they have any self-control? I get scared at fires. I don't bob my head up and scream like an infant.

"There's something else. I know you're new here and you don't understand our ways, but you need to keep your body covered."

"Is there something wrong with it?"

Is she playing stupid? My nerves were fraying like an old rope.

"There's something wrong with showing your boobs to men you don't know," I said.

"But I already met Willie."

"Damn it, Alana." I raised my voice. "You keep your fucking tits covered, okay? We've got enough trouble."

She nodded sadly. "Okay, Sam."

I slumped back onto the couch. I brought my fingers up and pinched the bridge of my nose. My back felt like I'd tumbled down a rockslide. I fidgeted to get a comfortable spot. My mind was a stew of anger. I had seen more death in a few days with Alana than in my last five years on the job. Obviously, it was dangerous to be in her vicinity.

My life was getting away from me and Alana was making it worse. If anybody saw me near where Sal's guys were killed, the word might get back and Fat Sal would hold me responsible. No way my dad was going to give me power of attorney since he caught me screwing Alana in the back room of his church. Sure, I had fifty grand in my trunk, but it was blood money. I'd promised Cindy that I'd make an effort to see Rae, but Alana was monopolizing all of my time.

I picked up the phone on the coffee table and punched in the number. "Hi, Cindy."

"You got some money for me, Sam?"

"Of course. Just got to get the time to drop it off."

"I'll come by."

"No, don't. It's not a good time for that. Give me a day or two."

"More time, Sam? Am I really gonna see this money?"

"Would it do any good to promise you that you will?"

"No."

I stood like a dummy listening to Cindy breathing. Finally she said,

"How's your pretty blonde friend?"

"Don't go there, please."

"I see. Someone else you let down."

"Can I just talk to my daughter for a little while?"

She called for Rae and I heard her little sweet pea steps racing over the carpet. "Hi, Daddy, I missed you. You been in any more fires? You be careful, okay? I tell all my friends about you. They're so jealous. How's Alana? I miss her, too. Tell her I want to see her soon." She went on in a four-minute run that melted my heart.

"Listen, darling," I told her. "I love you, too, but Daddy's got to go."

She hung up. I stared at the receiver, Rae's goodbye playing through my head.

"Tell her I said hi," Alana said. I looked over at her. She appeared to have collapsed into her sweatshirt; the tips of her fingers were peeking out of her sleeves, and her head had settled down into the hood.

"She hung up," I said.

"Oh."

"Don't you know how to use a telephone?" She shook her head. I motioned for her to sit next to me. "It would have helped if you had picked up at the warehouse. If it rings …." I showed her the workings. She turned the receiver around in her hand.

"Alana, I got to ask you. You know our language. You make love like a pro. How come you don't know how to wash your hair or use the phone?"

She shrugged. "I'm not sure. I'm not really an expert at traveling like this. I had to leave suddenly. But for some reason, language and the way people feel comes easy. The other stuff, I could learn it if we had enough time."

So the game plan stayed the same: keep her safe long enough for her people to find her, which hopefully would be before more bad guys showed up. We could have one night at Willie's. I didn't want to press him more than that for fear he'd lose his temper.

I stood up and threw my jacket around my shoulders.

"Where are you going?"

"Out on the porch. I just need to clear my head."

"Can I come?"

"I'd rather you didn't." I walked into the kitchen, flicked on the light, went into the fridge, and stuffed my pockets with six cans of beer. "I'll leave the light on in the kitchen, but not the one in the living room. Stay out of sight. I'll just be out front."

I could feel her mournful eyes following me as I walked out the door. The old wooden chair creaked when I dropped down into it. I zipped off the tab and took a long, cold drink.

I was angry at her for taking the blanket off, but I was angry at the whole thing. I didn't like seeing three guys get stomped to death, even if they *had* made my life miserable. I didn't like getting thrown around like a rag doll. I didn't like my best friend questioning me. I didn't like that he talked against Alana. And I really didn't like that I thought he was right.

I tried to pause my thoughts, to find a peaceful place in my head. I longed for a joint, but I knew Willie didn't keep any in his house. The beer went down easy, but it was hard to catch a buzz at four point five percent alcohol content.

If I kept Alana out of trouble for a little while longer, she'd be gone. She had to get back to save her planet or something like that. She'd been a little sparse on the specifics. It was easy to get carried away when she was around, but any pleasant time I'd spend with her would be just an interlude before I returned to my regular life. And anyway, I was used to strong Black women.

Twilight settled in. A pale light trickled through the trees. Occasionally a car zipped past. After the fourth beer, a bit of mellow came over me. I listened to every sound. From down the street a preteen thug-in-training shouted, "You're it," followed by the slap of two dozen sneakers against pavement, then excited arguments and laughs. Three houses down, across the street behind a chain link fence, a Doberman let out his raspy bark when a kid kicked a ball right past him.

A lilting chatter drifted through the air. I sat up and listened, then turned and looked through the picture window. In the shade of the living room, I saw Alana sitting on the couch. She held the phone to her ear.

I jumped up and pushed open the screen door. It rattled when it smacked the wall. I stood over her. She looked up to me and smiled and held up one finger. "It's Rae. She said to say hi."

I reached down and snatched the phone out of her hand. "Rae?"

"Hiya, daddy."

"How come you're on the phone?"

"Alana called me."

"Baby, I gotta go. You tell your mommy it's bedtime."

The receiver shook in my hand. I felt the blood rush to my face. "What the fuck are you doing, Alana?"

Her smile faded. She tilted her head down and glance up at me. "I just thought ...."

"You thought what?"

She seemed to sink into the couch cushions. "You were out there for a long time, and I was kind of scared, and I didn't know what to do. So I picked up the phone just to look at it. I didn't mean to call, but I must have hit the wrong button. Then I heard Rae's voice. We just talked, that's all."

She was like the kid who just had to touch the hot stove. Except now she'd brought my daughter into her drama. "Don't you ever think, Alana?"

"I ... I don't know what you mean."

"There are people who want to kill you. And it's three times now they've almost killed me when I was dumb enough to get in their way. Do you think it's a good idea to get my daughter involved in this?"

Her head dropped. "I just wanted to talk. I thought we could be friends."

I fought hard to keep control when what I really wanted to do was smack some sense into her. "You can't be friends with my daughter. You can't be friends with anybody. Don't you get it? Anybody you're in contact with could get killed."

"Okay," she squeaked.

I balled up my fists. "Fuck, Alana. My old friend Tony is dead. I hadn't seen him in years, and minutes after he runs into you, he's dead. My mom's friend Mona is dead. Three of Sal's guys. You know, I may not be much, but I try to protect people. At the end of the day, when everything else sucks, I can look back and say that maybe I did a little of God's work on this Earth and that someday when I stand before him, I can tell him that I ran into burning buildings and tried to keep people alive, and then he might be willing to give me a pass on some of the other stuff I've done."

"I'm sorry. I really am."

"You take guys like Willie and me, a couple of fuck ups. So you know what? We join the fire department and we're something. We drive down the street in the big red truck and people smile and wave. Kids beg us to hit the horn. People are glad to see us when we pull up to their house. Every day, a couple of losers like me and Willie get to do good."

She stretched her arm up to me and offered her hand. "I know you try to do good, Sam. That's why I chose you."

I swatted her hand away. She pulled it back quickly and tucked it under her armpit. "Do me a favor. Next time, pick somebody else." I tried not to, but now I was shouting. "You're a great piece of ass, but you're not worth getting killed over."

She wilted at my words.

"See that door?" I pointed to the spare bedroom off to the side. "I want you to stay in there. Turn on the television to keep yourself company. If you go to the bathroom, I want you to tell me so I can walk you there and back. But you stay in there until this goddamn nightmare is over."

She stood slowly and looked up at me, so unsteady I thought she might crumble. "Sam—"

"Go," I screamed. I had to let go of my anger somehow so I wouldn't yank her hair and swat her butt. She flipped the hood over her head, wrapped her arms around her shoulders, and shuffled toward the bedroom. At the door, she turned to me. The hood left the top of her face in shadow; her mouth and chin looked bone white. "I know I've been bad for you, Sam. But I promise you, if this works out for me, I'm going to make sure that things work out for you, too. I've been bad luck. I promised I would never lie to you, and I'll keep my word on this." She walked into the room and shut the door. I thought I heard her whimper but within seconds, any sound she might have made was drowned out by the television.

CHAPTER TEN

It took the rest of those six beers and a couple more to get me some sleep. It was a suds-in-the-gut sleep, the kind that always ends with jittery legs and bad dreams. As I rose into an unsettled semi-consciousness, I replayed my dilemma and what I'd said to Alana. I'd been harsh. My stomach turned over.

Our time together hadn't been all bad. I remembered the comforting feeling she'd given me at that fire, the serenity I'd experienced while I made love to her. Her vulnerability and kindness. Her glorious, unforgettable, heavenly face.

In my thoughts, every moment I shared with her passed by like a movie. It was pleasant at first, until I realized the pictures kept playing and I had no control over them. Like they were being dragged out of me. I heard a funny sound, as if all air was being sucked out of the room, and felt weightless, twirling without location, surrounded, suffocated, and erased. Something was taking me away from me.

I tensed my muscles, tried to feel the fabric of the couch, tried to focus on any sounds in the room. I fought to drive my fingernails into the palm of my hands. Finally, I felt pain that helped me wake from sleep—only to enter a nightmare reality. A malevolent pool of emerald flame surrounded me. It soaked into my pores, chomped into my skin, seeped into my mouth, and slithered into my nose. I wanted to cough it out. I wanted to scream, but the flame was thick and unyielding and consuming. Just when I thought I was lost, the green fire retreated to hang over me. Eyes formed and then the semblance of a face. The green faded and became brown; flames retreated, then configured into a nose and a mouth and ears. Muscles filled out its arms and shoulders. The face settled and the eyes bore down into me.

I looked up into myself.

Before I could make a sound, hands clamped down on my neck and cut off my breath. Uselessly, I thumped against tree trunk arms. The faces of Rae and Willie and Cindy and my father and Alana washed past me. My last thought before I lost consciousness was that I couldn't die because I'd be letting them all down.

***

I forced air through my sore throat and coughed in spasms. Pushing up and resting on my elbows, I looked around to orient myself. There I was, sitting across from me, looking back at me with amusement on my face—or, to be precise, on the face of whoever it was that looked exactly like me, the only difference being that he was much larger. He had pushed away the coffee table and moved the recliner right next to the end of the couch where I rested. A blue sweatshirt, with Engine 39 emblazoned in gold, stretched at the chest and shoulder. His biceps forced open the short sleeves.

I forced out words through my sore throat. "Who are you?"

"I guess I'm you, Sam. Let's just say I'm the new you, since I've only been here for about twenty minutes."

"Where's Alana?"

"Gone when I got here," he said. "I hope you don't mind that I looked through your memories. My God, Sam. You scared her half to death. That was stupid. Oh, and I helped myself to some of the old clothes in the drawer."

"Why ...," I stuttered, unsure of my question. It was unsettling to see my face looking down at me, to hear my own voice speaking to me.

"Why haven't I killed you? The thought crossed my mind. But then I thought, all this death. What has it gotten either of us?"

I tried to push myself up but he pressed his massive hand against my chest and forced me down. "Come on, Sam. Relax. We're just talking." He flipped something into my lap. The gun that Willie had given me. The barrel was twisted like a pretzel.

"What do you want from me?" I asked.

"I'm not sure." He brought his hands up in front of his face and turned them, studied them, then slapped them against his legs. "So curious, these forms of yours. Seems like you people went through a lot of trouble to come up with them. All these joints and cords and hormones. Very complicated. But then, that seems to be your nature. To make things more complicated than they really need to be."

"You've come to kill Alana."

"Let's examine that, shall we?" He sat back and brought his fingers together in front of his mouth. "This creature, Alana, pops up and says she needs help. You take what she says on faith. You agree to help her and resist us. Why? Because she's soft and alluring? Don't you think that's kind of dull witted? Is that the only way to attain anything in your world, to be sexually attractive? Remember, on my world she's a criminal. She stole something very valuable, something far more important than a few lives. And because she chose a form that provokes your tender feelings, you will do anything for her. Did you ever think that maybe she's the villain?"

"I know she's not."

"Come on. How do you know?"

"I can feel it from her."

"Don't be so gullible. I just looked into you and accessed all of your memories. Even copied your form. You have no capacity to do anything like that, but you claim to have a special intuition and that you must act accordingly. Let me ask you, do you know anything about my world?"

"Not much."

"Of course you don't. You don't know how we live, how we view right and wrong. Yet you dare to impose yourself into our internal affairs. Look at what happened to my kind on your world. We don't know what to wear, how to talk, what to eat, where to sleep. We stick out. We don't belong here. Your values puzzle us. Even though we are far stronger, our clumsiness allowed a wastrel like you to dispatch six of my kind."

"They were murderers."

"Is it murder to eliminate a criminal?" He smiled a big toothy smile. Were my teeth really that crooked? "We've had the capacity to come to your world for, well, you would consider it a very long time. But we rarely do. You know why? We don't fit in."

"What do you want from me?"

For a moment, he looked at me and kept the smile on his face. Then his hands moved too suddenly for me to react. One grabbed my balls, the other my neck. He squeezed with both. "I could kill you. I might even find that pleasurable. Or I might do it just to prove a point."

Pain flared up into my gut. I became weak and nauseous. I grabbed at his arms and uselessly tried to pull him away. He leaned next to my face and sneered. "Or I can just cause you pain. Break things one at a time. Maybe if you didn't have any balls you might be able to think straight."

"Don't."

"Don't what? Don't pull your balls off? Or don't kill Alana? I'll give you a choice. It's one or the other."

He squeezed harder. I felt like my nervous system short circuit. I couldn't focus or fight back.

"What's it gonna be, Sam?"

"Fuck you," I was able to force out.

He let go, threw back his head, and laughed. I grabbed my crotch, turned on my side, and moaned. He got to his feet. God, he must have been seven feet tall. He wore a pair of sweatpants that had fit Willie like a tent and now strained to contain his thighs.

"Damn it, Sam, I think I like you. Or maybe I like me. That's not weird, is it? All I'm asking is that you let your brain and not your reproductive glands do your thinking. I want you to consider what you are doing when you interfere in our internal politics. So far, we've left your planet alone. Frankly, we find it intensely boring. But if you resist us, you might pique our interest. That wouldn't be good for you."

He walked toward the door. On his feet, he wore Willie's winter overshoes. He pantomimed tossing a football. He turned back to me and smiled. "I bet I'd be really good at it. What do you think?"

"You couldn't hit water from the shore," I said.

He broke into a big smile. "Damn, this is going to be fun. Alana really picked the right guy."

"So I've been told."

"Just think about what you're doing, Sam. Don't let her play you for a fool." He walked out the door. The stairs creaked under his heavy steps. I tried to jump off the couch, but my legs felt like jelly. It took me a minute to stand and struggle to the front porch. I looked left and right, but under the streetlight were vacant sidewalks.

I felt empty. I couldn't do anything right. I was supposed to keep Alana safe, and now I had inflicted on her the worst enemy possible: the person who knows how she thinks, where she might go. And a version of me that has even less scruples than the original.

***

I drove through the deserted streets, using my fire department lantern to scan the sidewalks, houses, and vacant lots. Clutching a bottle, a raggedy old man shuffled down the sidewalk. From a block away, engines roared as a couple of young thugs raced down the street. Most people stayed in their houses on this chilly autumn evening.

I was searching for a ghost in a graveyard.

I got a queer feeling. Was I missing something obvious? Why hadn't he killed me? Why let me go so I could search the 'hood and find her before he could?

It came to me like a slap in the face. He copied me. He knew the way I thought.

He wants me to find her.

He's pressed for time. In his own cruel way, he wants to motivate me.

I pounded my temple with my fist. *Think, Sam. If I were him, what would I do?*

There was only one thing that would make me the most desperate man. The thing I feared the most. "Please, God, no."

I stomped on the accelerator. The car lurched forward and sped down the street.

In a few minutes, I parked in front of the well-kept two-story clapboard house. I flew out of the car and bounded up the steps. Before I could knock, a misty brown eye peeked out from the side of the door. It swung inward and Cindy stood in front of me. She trembled, unsteady on her feet, clinging to the door jamb.

"What does it all mean, Sam?"

"Where's Rae?"

"He took her. At first, I thought he was you. I mean, he looked like your older brother. But he was huge. He smiled, but his voice scared me."

I grabbed her by the arms. "Where did he take her?"

"He said he'd be in touch."

"Did you call the police?"

"He told me not to. He said if I did ...." She fell into my shoulder. "What does he want, Sam? We don't have any money. He's not going to hurt her, is he?"

I set my cheek against the top of her head and wrapped my arms around her. "I promise you he won't."

She shivered. *My poor beautiful Cindy. What have I done to you and our child?*

The phone rang. Cindy jumped out of my arms. I grabbed her wrist and nodded to her and she stepped back.

I picked up. "Hello?"

My voice, deep and cheerful, came over the phone. "Did you find the traitor yet?"

"I swear, if you hurt my daughter, I don't care how big you are, I will make you regret it."

"There's the Sam I know. Motivated. Alert. Adrenaline pumping, game time."

"Where are you?"

"Your daughter, what a little sparrow she is. So fragile. I am puzzled how you humans make it to adulthood. What soft skin covers her tender neck. The small bones, the supple cartilage that makes up her windpipe. What a tentative hold she has on life."

"What do you want?"

"Bring me the fugitive."

"Don't you think I'm looking?"

"You better look harder, because if I don't get Alana before she poofs away back to Ladallia, well, that means I came all the way across the galaxy for nothing. And I would be disappointed. Your little sweet pea here, I'll take her, but she might be just the start. I might take everything away from you, Sam. Then, just for kicks, let you live."

I looked at Cindy. Her arms were wrapped around her shoulders and her lips trembled.

"Tell me where you are," I said.

"I'll call the firehouse in an hour. Good luck in your search." I heard a click. There was no time to waste, but I froze. I was caught between two fire streams smacking against each other. A choice between two people I loved.

I felt Cindy's hand on my arm. "What should I do, Sam?"

I put the phone down and took her face in my hands. "You stay here. I know how to get her back. He's just a crazy cousin of mine. I don't think he means any harm."

"But—"

"Cindy, this may be hard for you, but you're going to have to trust me. I know that's not easy; I've let you down so many times before. But not this time. I promise you our daughter is coming back home safe and sound."

***

I cruised the side streets at twenty miles an hour in my creaky Crown Vic.

My stomach churned. Which was I, the hero or the creep? I had to put my daughter first. Even if it meant Alana. Even if it meant her entire planet.

Hell, Ladallia was a galaxy away. The entire world could go poof and it wouldn't make any difference to me. And I had no idea who was telling me the truth. Alana'd told me her story. Big Sam had told me his. And the whole thing was really none of my business. Sure, Alana was sweet and kind and the big guy was evil—at least, I thought so—but who was I to say how people should behave on Ladallia? It's wrong to look at a culture from the outside and pass a quick judgment.

Useless arguments clashed in my head. I knew if I betrayed Alana, it would haunt me for the rest of my life. But I had no choice.

I had to save my daughter.

Where would Alana go? I struggled to figure it out as I drove through the dark street.

I thought of what a strange and wonderful creature she was. How she could feel what I was thinking.

Alana didn't figure things out, she *felt*. I closed my eyes and thought of her, thought of where she might be, reaching out with my mind. A picture formed, and I sped off into the night.

***

The Crown Vic sidled up to the mess that was formerly the Central Park Plaza, the place where Alana had first appeared. Three ruts scored the pavement from one side of the plaza to the other. With lantern in hand, I got out. I forced open the gate and it screeched. The beam followed the trenches. Moonlight flickered over the broken buildings.

My lantern swept left, and I noticed a form, tall and thin, gliding over the upturned blacktop. I waited. My mouth went dry. I wanted to run to her and snatch her in my arms, but I swallowed and forced myself to stay cool.

She came over to me, glanced up quickly, then tilted her face downward.

"Hi, Sam."

I couldn't tell if she was happy to see me or angry that I'd yelled at her. Or maybe she knew that, as much as I wanted to help her, I intended to lead her to her death because I had to save my daughter. I couldn't get a read on her.

"You want to go for a ride?"

She nodded.

"There's another one, isn't there?" she asked.

"Yes."

I opened the door for her and she slid in. I shivered as cold wind whipped through her broken window and reached me on the other side. She pulled the drawstring of her hood so I could only see her nose.

"Where are you taking me?"

"The firehouse."

"I understand."

We rode in silence.

***

We got there at one in the morning. Willie sat at the table, his feet resting on a chair, his hand tapping the ashes of a cigarette into the ashtray. Alana kept her hood on and went to the far corner of the kitchen to stand in front of the stove we kept lit on cold nights because the firehouse heating system sucked.

"Hey, Willie."

"You're like a fucking bad penny," he growled.

"Quiet night?"

"Sure, if you don't count those green ruts we keep finding all over the place. Another one appeared in Martin Luther King Park."

The one Big Sam used for his entrance, no doubt.

"Alana and I need to stay here. It's just for a little bit."

"Suit yourself," Willie said. "It's your firehouse, too."

Big Daddy walked into the room in a T-shirt that barely covered his middle, boxers, and slippers. "Whoa," he said, and turned on his heels back into the apparatus floor.

"Rich," I called, "it's okay. We ain't staying too long."

"You look lovely anyways," Willie said.

He came back a moment later wearing his fire turnout pants, his red suspenders straining at his big shoulders.

"Sorry, Miss," Rich said. "I apologize that I have to share the firehouse with a couple of baboons." He sat down next to Willie.

"The phone free? I'm expecting a call," I said.

"Free and clear," Rich said.

We sat in uncomfortable silence. Alana reached out her hands so they were close to the stove. Rich got up and walked over to her. "Sorry my friends got no manners. You wanna sit? How about some coffee?" He guided her to the table. She sat near the window, opposite from Willie and me.

She declined the coffee. The television blared out a music video. The radiator made a series of empty clicks. The hand on the clock jerked as it punctuated the seconds. After a moment, Rich spoke. "I'm not missing anything, am I? Did somebody die?"

"Yeah," Willie said. "Your fucking drawers died of ass poisoning and you should bury them. You know they come three to a pack."

"I like to wear them 'til they get a life of their own."

I stood up. "I'm gonna wait by the phone. I don't want to miss my call."

The apparatus floor was about twenty degrees warmer. Two rows of radiators lined the wall and the safety valve hissed steam. Gray dirt spoiled the bright red finish of the rig. On its open doors hung fire coats and helmets.

I paced back and forth in front of the phone booth. I'd done my part. I found Alana. Now I wanted my daughter back. I wanted it to be a week in the future, where I'd paid off Fat Sal and distributed some cash to Cindy. I wanted to walk Rae to the park down the street from their house. We'd hold hands and Rae would chatter away. I'd push her on the swing and stand by the slide with my arms outstretched to catch her if she fell. Everything back to normal, everything taken care of.

I just wouldn't know what to say when she asked about Alana.

My mind raced. I thought of football games that I should have won, how I should have called in sick the day of the fire truck flipped over, and how I should have handled things better with Cindy. I pictured my time with Alana and I knew it would haunt me until the day I die.

Finally, the phone rang. I shouted, "I got it," and lunged, snatched the heavy black receiver and held it to my ear.

"Sam! What's the good news?"

I leaned in and held my hand over the mouthpiece. "I got her."

"I knew you would. She's drawn to you, like she's repelled by me."

"Let me speak to Rae."

My palms began to sweat. My baby's voice was shrilled with terror. "Daddy, I'm so scared."

"Daddy's coming for you, darling. Everything is going to be all right."

"Touching," he said.

"Promise me you won't hurt her. Promise me or you'll never see Alana."

"I have no interest in staying on this hellhole world one minute longer than I have to. Bring the criminal to me and you can take your daughter home."

"Where?"

"That warehouse where the first two fell. I'll be with your precious Rae on the third floor."

"We'll be there in ten minutes."

"Remember, Sam. If you bring anybody besides the two of you, if you sneak a weapon in your coat, I'll have my fingers around your daughter's neck. It's hard to hold a sparrow in your hand for long without hurting it."

I slammed down the phone and pushed through the door to the kitchen.

Willie sat next to Alana by the foot of the table. Her hood down, her golden hair exposed, she spooned a piece of apple pie into her mouth while Willie bobbed his head and chuckled. Rich sat next to her, filling his own face.

I stood over them.

"Skinny as she is, this girl sure can eat," Willie said.

"We need to go, Alana."

Alana stood, and Willie and Rich followed suit. "I'm glad we got to talk a little bit," she said. "Sam has wonderful friends." She bent down and kissed Big Daddy on the crown of his bald head.

She turned to Willie, who reached out his hand. "I guess you're all right," he said. Alana threw her arms around his neck and held on. I swear I saw Willie blush. He hugged her back, then patted her shoulder. "Go on now." Then he turned his eyes on me. "You keep her safe, Sam."

***

We cruised down the dark street. The temperature had dipped close to freezing and swooped in from the broken window, overwhelming the prodigious heater of the Crown Vic. Alana kept her distance from me.

"What did you say to Willie?" I had to speak loudly to be heard over the air rushing in.

She kept looking straight ahead. "I don't know what you mean."

"Well, he was all pissed off at you when he left the house."

She nodded. "I didn't want him to be mad at me. Especially if I don't get to see him again. I told him I thought he was wonderful and brave. I told him I knew he was a good man. I told him he was so lucky to have you and Rich as friends."

It was the perfect thing to say. Maybe too perfect.

"That worked like a charm," I said. "And you got some apple pie out of it."

I turned down Main Street and passed my father's church. She craned her neck to look at it.

"It looks kind of scary in the dark," she said.

"We haven't been able to take care of it. When it's all fixed up and lit the way it should be, the building is really very beautiful."

"Can I ask you something, Sam?"

"Why not?"

"Tell me about Jesus."

I looked at her. Why did she want to bring Jesus into this? Was she trying to make me feel guilty?

I could have recited something from my father's sermons. I could have given her some vague, non-commital answer. Instead, I stuttered, choking on my words. Me, the guy who always had an answer.

"Sam?"

Maybe I could tell her how I woke up every day and hoped things would get better; that every night, I wondered why I'd even tried. I could shout at her, tell her that I didn't believe in God. Because, obviously, he didn't care about me, not one little bit.

"I didn't mean to upset you."

I realized I was shaking. "What the hell *did* you mean then?"

"We have things like that on Ladallia. I guess you call it religion. It's nice to have something to believe in."

I was hanging from a ledge by my fingertips. I couldn't waste time on old words and silly rituals.

She pointed at a vacant lot where a nursery used to be. "See that?"

"They used to sell plants there," I said. "A long time ago." Now all that remained was a brick building falling in on itself and a field full of weeds hemmed in by a rusty old fence.

"Picture trees and flowers, mothers watching their children play in the grass."

"It's just another piece of ghetto that nobody wants."

"Picture something nice. Try to believe in it. Before anything changes, we have to picture it."

"I can't."

"We've all got to believe in *something*, Sam."

Her words hurt. I wanted to lash out at her and say, "Nobody makes a fool of Sam Carver." But that great reservoir of energy that I had used to win football games and rush into fires drained out of me. Because she was right. It wasn't God I didn't believe in.

I didn't believe in me.

***

I drove past the college bars. Lines stretched fifty deep outside for a chance to get in. Get drunk. Get laid. It hadn't changed since I was in college when life was just a good buzz and getting your rocks off. Until sometime down the line they turned into somebody like me.

I made the turn down the street where Rich had his rental property, where Alana had stayed. We passed the sidewalks where she'd made her desperate flight to the tower, where I'd desperately chased her, when I would have done anything to save her.

"Sam."

"Yes, Alana."

"I want you to know something. I may seem stupid to you sometimes, but that's because I don't know how things work. But I'm smart when it comes to feelings."

Up ahead was the side street that led into the yard with the abandoned tower. In spite of the cold outside, perspiration collected under my hands where I clutched the wheel.

"You're a good man, Sam. You think that people see you as a screw-up. But that's not it. You see yourself that way. To make things better, you only have to start believing in yourself."

How can I believe in an empty shell?

I made the turn. The tower loomed over the yard. The full moon left one side in silver and the other in shadow. The Crown Vic popped up and down on the uneven pavement.

"I know you're trying," she said.

The moonlight turned her skin to porcelain. Her eyes flashed like eternity.

"You're trying to do the right thing. I would never be mad at you for that."

"Alana ...." The rest of my sentence stuck in my throat. I'd been able to talk myself through any kind of trouble. Now I saw that they were just words. Worthless words.

A green flash cut across the windshield. I slammed on the brakes, and Alana darted out the door. I reached for her, but too late. She walked in front of the car where there stood a green flame, as tall as she was, roughly in the form of a man. As she stood next to it, her skin started to shine. Green, hot and powerful. The emerald energy enveloped her and increased in intensity. I thought she'd become like him. They'd float away, back to Ladallia, and I'd never see her again. She'd be safe.

And Rae would end up dead.

I wanted to do something, but nothing I thought of made sense. There was nothing I could say to her. If I were in her shoes, I'd leave. I know I would.

Then the green light faded and she was alone, with normal-colored skin and golden hair, wearing a green hoodie that was two sizes too big. She opened the door and slid back into the car, this time scooching next to me and leaning her head against my shoulder. "Keep driving, Sam."

"I don't understand," I said.

"We've got to save Rae."

"But the green light, it came for you, didn't it?"

"I told him I can't leave like this."

"Your planet ...."

"They've been fighting there for a very long time. Whether I go back or not, I guess they'll keep on fighting."

"The one they sent, he wants to kill you."

"I know."

I wanted to melt into the seat. "I don't know what to say."

Her long fingers wrapped around my arm. She rubbed her cheek against my jacket. "Just don't leave me, okay? Stay with me until the end."

CHAPTER ELEVEN

At one hundred feet the lot was too littered with junk for my Crown Vic to get any closer. I helped her out of the car. The wind whipped through the open field, piercing my jacket, and stinging my ears. We walked and Alana took my hand. Her fingers were ice cold. I steadied her as we made our way over the uneven ground, the railroad ties and discarded tires.

The fire escape lay in a heap by the side of the building. It had been creaky when I'd climbed it. But whatever tore it down had to have been incredibly powerful. Like Big Sam.

The same monster who had his hand around my daughter's throat.

The door was stuck open about a foot. I wiggled through. Alana followed. The concrete floor seemed to suck the heat right through my sneakers. The wind meandered through the cracks and windows.

I wrapped my arm around her shoulders. She was so frail and thin. We took the stairs. The rotting steps groaned. The sides of the staircase were open. Our heads peeked through the level of the second floor. In front of us, as big as a hot tub, was a sloppy pile of wood shavings. Heaps of frayed newspapers and stacks of gray lumber were scattered through the room. A bank of barrels three high sat rusting against one wall, their labels too faded to reveal what they contained.

Rae didn't belong in a place like this. She should have soft grass under her bare feet, her teddy bear cuddled under her arm, her blanket pulled up to her chin. This place threatened with old rotting dead things.

The crisp night air mixed with a moldy odor.

Even though we were protected from the wind, the inside of the building felt like an icebox. We made the turn at the second landing. Alana slowed, her legs shaky, as if she had to force each step. Her hand clenched mine desperately. I heard the crackling and saw the red glow on the next landing. Didn't that crazy alien know how easily this dried out old building would light up? Before our heads came to floor level, she looked at me, forced a smile, and mouthed the words "I love you."

She loved me. There were too few people like that in my life. Rae, Willie, Rich. Who else? I realized that I loved her, too, and it wasn't because of her emerald eyes or that she looked like a nymph or that she made love like it was her life's work, or even that she resembled Farrah

Fawcett. She could have been made of mud. I would have still loved her for being a good soul. I knew I had found a friend.

So far, I had hoped and prayed. But God helps those who help themselves. There had to be something I could do. The game wasn't over. There was still time on the clock.

We peered over the level of the floor. In the left corner was the source of the red light: a barrel with a few sticks of charred lumber poking out of the top, tongues of flame darting, snapping, and crackling. Behind the barrel, bathed in red, sat Big Sam, shivering, one hand around my daughter's neck. They sat on a bundle of old rags that were bound with metal bands.

"Why did you tear down the fire escape?" I asked.

He stood up. "Couldn't have anybody sneaking up on us."

"Daddy, I want to go home," Rae said. Her lower lip trembled.

"We're going home soon, darling," I said. Then to Big Sam I said, "You must be crazy, starting a fire in here. This place could go up like a flare."

"It's this miserable planet," he said. "My clothes are all wrong."

"I guess you don't know everything."

"I know enough. Give her to me" he said, and nodded to Alana, "so I can get out of this hellhole." He heaved himself up. His biceps were as big as my thighs and his left hand easily encircled Rae's throat.

Alana stepped toward him; I pulled her back. "First let Rae go."

"Once I get my hands on the fugitive, you can have your daughter."

"I don't trust you."

"We'll exchange," he said, "at exactly the same time."

The embers flicked out of the bucket. To me it had *dangerous fire* written all over it. But Big Sam paid no mind. I watched the embers rise in the air and scatter through the room. He stared at Alana, stretched out his hand.

He had used my memories but still hadn't put everything together. The cold, the possibility of fire, he was oblivious to the obvious.

An idea came to me and I tried not to smirk.

"At the same time, then," he said. "Come here, Alana." He reached out for her, his greedy hand opening and closing. Alana stepped forward, tipped her head back, and held her neck straight. True to my promise to her, I kept my hand on her arm.

"Now," Big Sam said. Alana stopped in front of him. He let Rae go and clamped down on Alana's neck. Rae slid off the bundle and ran into my leg.

Alana's eyes closed. She grabbed at his wrist. Her lips moved but no sound escaped.

"So sweet. Another little bird in my hand."

I walked casually to his right side. "One thing," I said.

He looked at me, the grin still on his face.

"Are you getting used to this body?"

"What are you talking about?"

"I was wondering when you were going to find out about my bad back." I turned sideways, picked up the foot closest to him and drove my heel into his hip, right on the weak spot that had haunted me since I fell off the fire truck. There was a crack and his hips shifted to one side. He bellowed, fell—and let go of Alana. He reached for his back and rolled on the floor. The lip of the barrel scorched my hands when I grabbed it and toppled the contents on top of him. The flames shot up excitedly and he bellowed again.

I grabbed Alana and Rae's hands and ran for the stairs. His howl haunted the room. I turned at the sound of a hollow crunch. He'd kicked the barrel right at us. I tugged on Ray and Alana's wrists. The barrel spit out fire and wobbled by and missed them by inches. At the stairway, it tumbled down end over end. I ran to the landing and watched it smash against the wood shavings. Bits of wood shot up in the air and morphed into angry red fireflies. It only took a second for the entire mass to catch fire.

Big Sam cursed and pushed himself up. The oil, rags, and rubber in the barrel were scattered over the lower stairwell. With Alana and Rae in hand, I took two steps down the stairs. The shavings spit fire at our faces. I pulled them back.

Big Sam took one step toward us and slammed face first on the deck. He cursed and smashed the floor with his fist. He crawled after us with surprising quickness. I threw Rae up to my shoulder, pulled Alana's hand, and hurried up the steps.

Going up would buy us some time. But the only way out was down and that was blocked by a giant alien monster and a shitload of fire.

We reached the fourth-floor landing. I heard him curse again and felt his hand on my ankle. I fell on my back, coiled my other leg, and kicked him in the top of the head. He slid back down to the lower landing.

We'd made it to the fifth floor when I heard the cackle of the fire. I knew that crazy song by heart. Heat must be rolling over and chewing up soft wood, paper, and rags. Soon it would spread to those abandoned barrels.

Alana took the stairs with her light steps and waited for me at each landing, lending her meager strength by pulling on my shirt. Rae buried her head against my neck.

I looked back. He'd gained ground.

At the sixth floor, my own back started to ache. I shifted Rae to my right side and used my free arm to yank on the handrails. Smoke drifted up. A crimson spotlight shot up from below to show us that the fire was gaining hold.

Seven floors up, we came to the roof. I looked back to see Big Sam turning the corner. I rammed into the door of the tower. The hinges squawked. The door moved slowly. Alana threw her shoulder against it, as did Rae. Finally, the rust surrendered with a bark, the door swung open, and we were on the roof. Big Sam shouted. Looking around frantically, I found a crowbar and wedged it through the hasp of the now-closed door. I stood back. The door shuddered and the crowbar rattled as he machine-gunned his fists against the door.

"I'm going to kill you, Sam. All of you."

I told Alana to find a place to hide. She ran to some barrels in the corner, bent down and threw her arms around my daughter. They shivered together, in the moonlight, a study in silver and gray. I ran to the edge. A gust of wind whipped up the side of the building and slashed against my face. Down the way, Main Street was lined with slow moving white and red lights. I scanned down the street, where Truck 34, the nearest fire company, was housed, hoping I to see the red and yellow lights of their gumball headed our way. But looking down at the lot below, the darkness told me we were all alone.

Boom! The roof rocked. Rae screamed. I looked over the side and saw gouts of flame spitting out of the lower windows of the building. The fire must have touched off those barrels; whatever they contained blew up really well.

Big Sam pounded and cursed.

I hurried around the perimeter of the building, drawing into my lungs gobs of dry ice air. Flame out spit out of every second-floor window.

We had some time until the fire reached us, or until Big Sam broke down the door. But there was no place to go. If the stairs burned through, nobody could rescue us from within.

The roof was full of garbage: empty buckets, lumber that was black with rot, sheets of fiberglass panels nailed to two by fours. I looked around for something to use as a weapon.

From the other side of the door the pounding stopped. "I'm coming for you, Sam. You son-of-a-bitch. I should have known. You're a fighter, damn it. Times running out, though."

"Fire's going to take the whole building," I shouted. "This way, we're all going to die."

"I guess that's how it's got to be," he said. "You didn't think I'd be afraid, did you? I learned from the best."

The only thing I could find for a weapon was a four-by-four piece of pressure treated lumber, maybe five feet long. It was way too heavy and hard to get a grip on.

The pounding resumed. A trickle of smoke snuck out of the sides of the door and wended its way skyward.

I looked at where Alana and Rae were hunkered down behind a short stack of buckets. Alana's straight hair and Rae's curly puff were barely visible.

I leaned next to the hinge side of the door, holding the four-by-four like a bat. The screws holding the door to the hinges tittered with every blow. Finally the door exploded out, twirled, and skidded across the roof. Smoke rushed out with Big Sam.

My makeshift club slammed against his skull. He fell to all fours. I raised the board high over my head ad stretched up on my toes. I wanted to crush his skull.

His arm shot up. The board stopped cold and reverberated in my hand. It felt as if I'd slammed it against concrete. He yanked the board away from me and tossed it over the side. A sliver bit into the soft cushion of my palm. He swatted me across the temple and I rolled across the roof, the stones like little darts poking through my jacket.

He lurched for me, screamed, and toppled to his knees. As I had done many times since my accident, he moaned and held the painful spot on his back. I scrambled to my feet and put distance between us. He pushed up, his face twisted in pain, but with his back out of whack, he had trouble standing. I didn't think he'd ever be able to catch me. He turned and limped toward Alana and Rae.

"Stay out of his way," I yelled. Alana grabbed Rae's hand and they ran to the other side of the tower.

The pattern was obvious. Big Sam couldn't catch us. When he ventured too far from the door, I moved toward it and he retreated to cover it.

There was another boom. The roof shook and seemed to drop several feet on one side. I waved my arms and tried to keep my balance. The building settled with a groan and now canted a few feet toward the street.

"This is crazy," I yelled.

"You're not getting out of here, Sam," he said. His sweatshirt was singed. Raw pink burn marks dotted his face and bare arms.

"This doesn't make any sense," I said. "Let's all get down."

"I can't go back. She has to die."

"Then stay on Earth. At least you'll be alive."

"They'll chase me," he said, "just like her. Better to end it all right here."

I tried not to look, but it was too spectacular of a sight. I saw a green star high in the heavens. It twinkled like an emerald then descended slowly, becoming brighter, growing. Alana's people were coming for her.

But where would that leave my precious Rae?

Big Sam snapped his head around. "Damn them," he said. He limped away from the door to a pile of old rusty buckets. I knew what they were: some sloppy contractor had left them behind. When full, they carried fifty pounds of roofing tar. Even empty, they had to go at least fifteen pounds. Big Sam picked one up, reared back, and flung it toward Alana and Rae.

Rae screamed. The bucket whistled through the air and hit the roof a few feet in front of them. It bounced left, then right, and zoomed over their heads and smashed against the parapet wall.

Good God. He threw like me times five.

Big Sam stepped closer to them, another bucket cocked behind his head. This one was a dead on, but Rae and Alana moved to the side at the last second and the missile skidded over the side.

Alana pushed Rae. "Go to your daddy." Rae scampered along the perimeter, taking the long route so that she stayed away from Big Sam. I wanted to rush to Alana, but Rae clung to my leg.

He grabbed another bucket As if to test its heft, he tossed it up in the air a few inches, then turned toward Alana, stepped forward, and grunted. The bucket sizzled in a tight spiral. Alana tried to move, but caught her foot on some trash and the bucket smashed into her leg. The crack was sickening. She moaned and toppled over.

He made his way to Alana, more hopping than walking.

Rae and I had a straight shot for the door. Smoke rolled out of the top of the opening. We had to leave now to have any chance.

In the distance, I heard my favorite song: the roar of sirens. Two rigs turned into the yard.

Big Sam brought up his foot. Alana rolled to the side. He lost his balance and fell on all fours. Alana tried to push herself up. Her sweatpants were ripped from hip to knee. Her blood looked black as it poured out of her leg.

I could not leave her.

"Don't move, Rae," I said. I picked up the crowbar that lay next to the door. Big Sam shuffled after Alana, reached down for her as she tried to crawl behind a pile of tires. I pushed for them as fast as I could. The sound of destruction crackled through the openings of the building. Big Sam was inches away from her. I smashed the crowbar down on his shoulder. He stumbled. I struck again but he turned to me quickly and only took a glancing blow to his massive neck. His hands were on my jacket and I was off my feet. My fists thumped against his wrists. I tried to land a kick into his face.

"Run to the stairs," I shouted to Alana.

She moaned. "I can't feel my leg."

Big Sam shoved me and I sailed weightless through the crisp air of dark sky and piercing stars. I wildly swung my arms to snag something, desperately trying to hang on to some hope. I plopped against the asphalt. I thought my rib cage collapsed.

Finally my arms worked, and I pushed against the cold pitch and stones beneath me. My tortured back shrieked out pain. I rolled, got my limbs under me.

He held Alana above him, his hands on her neck. Blood dripped down her leg. Her cracked femur poked through the rip in her pants. She slapped her hands against his arms, over and over, slower and slower, as her energy drained away.

I stumbled forward and picked up the crowbar. It felt like it weighed fifty pounds. I lowered the blade end to use it like a spear. He glanced over his shoulder and swatted at me backhand. He swung high; I ducked, and brought the bar down on his hand.

There was a crack. He pulled his hand away, studying the misshapen thumb while still holding on to Alana with the other hand. Then he swung at me and his forearm whizzed over my head. I lost my footing and fell onto a bucket. I imagined that was what an alligator biting into my sore ribs would feel like.

"You're a pain in the ass, Sam," he said. "Now watch her die."

His forearm muscles ripple. Alana looked straight up, then closed her eyes. Her arms fell to her side.

"No," I screamed.

She looked so precious in the moonlight, washed out of color except for a tint of gold in her hair. All her parts hung so innocently, her long fingers, her trim legs, which could have been from some elegant marionette fit for a royal performance were they not marred by the gash in her thigh.

Big Sam exhaled, turned to me, and smiled. I couldn't turn my eyes away from what was happening to Alana.

A form of green flame shot down from the sky and hovered over her, reached down as if it had an arm and a finger, and touched her on the top of the head. Alana's eyes snapped open and glared at Big Sam. A patina came to her skin which made her shine, then glow, then finally flare out in sizzling energy. She raised her arms to her sides, palms up toward the heavens. I smelled the ozone smell of electricity, then, with a poof, she was a green flame through and through. She floated up, up, until the last thing I could make out was a broad smile across her face and her eyes looking into mine.

Big Sam howled as the twin green flames twirled in the air before shooting out of sight.

"Too late," I said.

He looked down at me, his face twisted in hate. Then he turned and limped across the roof. I wanted to laugh at him until I realized that Rae was peeking around the tower wall.

I shouted, "Run," but it came too late. He snatched her up with one hand and hobbled to the side of the building.

I forced myself up, ignoring every pain, and ran. He was a few steps from the side of the building when he wound up as if he were ready to throw a pass. "Please," I shouted, "take me. She's got nothing to do with this."

He stopped right at the edge and turned back to me one more time. "I know this is going to hurt you, Sam. But I have to do it. If you knew us better, you'd understand why."

He brought Rae up to his ear. I screamed, a mere few feet away, stretching out for my daughter who hung in the air, framed by the stars, flailing her tiny limbs.

Green lightning streaked across his face. He grunted and brought his hands in front of his eyes. Rae fell to the roof. Like a little cat, she landed on her feet and scrambled away.

Thank you, Alana. Thank God for you.

I lowered my shoulder and hit him in the small of the back. He groaned and reached behind, his hands hungry for a piece of me. I drove my fist into his kidney. He teetered and his feet jammed against the parapet. I felt him lose his balance. I churned my legs, tried to sink my toes into the tar for a foothold.

But it wasn't enough. He was able to turn and I pushed helplessly into a mountainside. My legs pumped, but they lost their strength and I sagged. If I wasn't leaning against him, I probably would have fallen.

His hand clamped on my neck. From the level of his chest, I looked up to his face, to his twisted grin, to the raw meat spots that spoiled his complexion.

"Game over, Sam," he said.

With all the strength I could muster, I drove my fist into his groin. He doubled over, clutching himself.

"Overtime, motherfucker." I slammed into his chest with everything I had. He fell back. His arms windmilled, hands snatching at my shirt, but he couldn't catch hold. I dove into him again. He teetered and started to fall into the background of red and yellow lights from the fire trucks.

I thought I'd won. I tried to step back, but with a swipe of his long arm, he caught the collar of my jacket with one finger. He jerked me forward and suddenly there was no roof under my feet. The contents of my stomach threatened to part ways with me. I lost sight of him as we fell through smoke.

My life couldn't end like this, with Rae stuck on the roof and no way for her to get down. I had saved Alana but left my daughter to die. One step forward, two steps back. That's how it always was for me.

I felt a sizzle and suddenly I was surrounded by green flame. It was beautiful. My regrets drained away. I never should have doubted the girl from outer space.

Then I stirred. I felt like I was about to slough Alana off of me.

"Rae ...."

She's going to be all right.

I don't know why, but I believed it. I relaxed into a green cushion, halfway between my world and hers. Around me, I heard the muffled blare of sirens. I barely made out violent orange tongues slurping out of the windows of the tower. The stomping of boots and the urgent voices sounded far away. I sunk into a wonderful dream of emerald rivers and golden flowers.

***

I came to with an oxygen mask over my mouth. I pushed myself up to my elbows. Against my face, I felt heat like the noonday sun in mid-July. Flames belched out of the windows, coughed through doorways, flicked out of every possible opening, and danced over the roof. No one could survive in that.

I pulled the mask off my face. "Rae?"

"You need to chill, Sam." It was Rich, in his turnout gear, his helmet sitting on his melon head. "We thought we lost you."

I tried to get up, but he forced me back down. "Ain't nothing you can do there, cousin."

I grabbed at his wrists and looked him in the eye. "You don't understand. My daughter..."

"Daddy!" I heard her cry, and it was the best sound I'd ever heard. She ran to me and threw her arms around my neck.

I grabbed her head in my hands and studied her wide-set chestnut eyes, her turned up nose, and her heart-shaped lips. I took a moment to make sure it was really her before I pressed her against my chest. "My beautiful girl."

She pulled away and ran her fingers under my eyes. "Don't cry, Daddy. Alana said it would be all right, so I wasn't afraid. And then I saw them." She pointed to Willie. He pulled off his tank and took a drink of water.

"Willie," I shouted. "You crazy son-of-a-bitch."

He trudged over and plopped down in the dirt right next to me. "Crazy shit, Sam. Really crazy shit."

"How the hell did you do it?"

"We pulled up next to the hook and ladder." Willie shook his head. "I don't get it. Maybe I'm getting old. Maybe our district is haunted. I don't know how to tell you this without you thinking I've gone pots."

"I already think you're pots."

"Damn." He shook his head again. "I got off the rig to size up the building. Then I saw a thing."

"What kind of thing?" Although I could have guessed.

"Something flashed in front of my face. Like lightning. Except it was green. And at that moment, I was sure that Rae was up on the roof. What the fuck would she be doing up there? But I was sure of it."

I chuckled. "Good call."

"So I start screaming that we got to get the aerial ladder up to the roof. The captain of the truck company thinks I'm crazy. Everybody thinks I'm crazy, including me. But I was sure of Rae needing us on that roof if I was ever sure of anything. So the captain tells me no way is he putting the ladder up because the building is lost and if the ladder gets fucked up he's got to write a mess of reports. So I start cussing."

"I bet that helped."

"I'm cussing like a madman. Everybody's looking at me. Rich, the big lug, is patting my back telling me to calm down. So did Al."

"You can always count on our L.T. to be useless."

"That's the thing, Sam. I thought I was going to have to raise the aerial myself and fight two companies to boot. But Al looks at me, and I know he gets it. So he starts cussing at the captain, saying if someone dies on that roof and we don't try then it's on his sorry ass. Then Rich joins in. The captain throws up his hands. We raise the aerial. And Al and I brought down Rae."

Rae raised her hand to her mouth to stifle a laugh. "Uncle Willie doesn't know what the green fire is for."

I threw my arm around Willie's shoulder. "I love you, ya big lug."

"If Al didn't stand up for me like he did, it might have been different," Willie said. He nodded to the rear running board of Engine 27, where Al sat watching the fire, his helmet at his side, and a peaceful smile on his face.

"And I couldn't have asked for a better backup on the roof. Except you, of course. Al stayed with me all the way."

To the side was a bare patch where it looked like a small bomb had exploded. Willie nodded at it. "You got any idea what made that?"

"Can't say."

"You got any explanation why my sweatshirt and boots were there, right in the middle?"

"Probably not."

"Why the fuck Rae was on the top of the building? How come you ain't dead? You want to answer me, or you want to wait until I ask you about fifty more questions?"

"It's complicated," I said.

"I get it. How about you don't tell me? 'Cause I got a feeling what comes next is a steaming crock of horse shit."

"One of these days," I said. "Maybe over a beer."

"Maybe over a liter of Crown Royal," he said.

CHAPTER TWELVE

Cindy was so happy to see Rae that she only reminded me a couple of times that this was all my fault. We sat together on the couch until sunup, with our daughter curled up between us, her breath puffing out in gentle snores. Then we put Rae to bed. I grabbed Cindy's hand. She pulled away and turned her back to me.

"Don't do that," she said.

"Cindy, if you let me explain."

"I'm sorry, Sam. I don't want to hear any more explanations."

"But this wasn't my fault."

"It never is. Don't get me wrong, Sam. I know you're trying to do the right thing. But I just can't live like this. You do something wrong, then you scramble to straighten it out. Remember that gang fight they had at the park a few months ago, where that fourteen-year-old girl was shot in the head while she was in her own kitchen doing her homework?"

"What has that got to do with us?"

"The newspapers said the girl was collateral damage to a gang war. I can't allow Rae to be exposed to that."

"I'd die before I let anybody hurt you or my daughter."

She turned to me and brushed her hand against my face. "Oh, Sam. I know you would. You're brave and strong. I know you love us. But with all the stuff that goes on around you, I just can't let Rae and I be collateral damage."

I had no energy to argue. I dropped an envelope with fourteen thousand dollars on the bookshelf. I stopped at the door and looked back. "I'm sorry, Cindy. Sorry for everything." I walked down the steps to my car.

I was dead tired but there were a couple of things I had to handle before I could lay my head down. From Cindy's, I went right to the restaurant on the west side where I knew Fat Sal communed daily with the local mob and a stack of pancakes. I walked inside. The odor of coffee and bacon activated the hunger in my gut. The tables had red and white checkerboard tablecloths. Italian types argued and gestured with their hands. From the rear corner, Fat Sal fixed his eyes on me with a stony look and chewed at the same time, then flicked his head toward the back room.

At his desk, his tune changed when he thumbed through the thirty-five large I dropped in front of him.

He counted. A guy stood behind me while he did.

Sal neatly stacked the money in piles in front of him.

I said, "So we're good?"

He sat back in his chair and folded his sausage fingers over his protruding belly. "Strange things, Sam. I lost three guys. Did you know that?"

"Sorry to hear it."

"Yeah. Three guys who happened to be looking for you. I tried to put two and two together when someone who knew somebody who saw what happened said that my guys were beaten to death. By three naked white guys. You got any explanation for that?"

"Doesn't make any sense, Sal."

"No, it don't. Naturally, I suspected you. But that didn't add up either. Seein' you got the money." He bit his lower lip. "I hear you lost somebody, too."

I nodded.

He swiveled his chair to the side and looked out the window. "Mona and me," he said, "we go way back. We'd call each other. She told me about you. She said she liked you, said the worst thing to do was to lend you money. She was good people. I'm sorry she's gone."

"Me, too."

He stroked his stomach and got a dreamy look on his face. "Damn, that woman was quite a looker in her day."

"Sal?"

He smacked his lips and shook his head.

"You two didn't by any chance ...."

He quickly stood and waved his hand toward the door. "We're done. I'm gonna take Mona's advice, Sam. I ain't gonna lend you any more money no matter how much you beg."

"I would consider that a favor."

***

Next stop was the former Church of the New Jerusalem. I sat in the front row, in the exact spot where I used to sit next to my mother while we listened to my dad preach. I recalled how Dad's voice would start out like a lamb in pasture and rise to the volume of fire roaring out of hell. I remembered the women in their fancy flowered dresses, their wrists like dumplings, white gloves on their hands. They would fan themselves, raise their arms, and shout out hallelujah. How the men in black suits with sweat dripping off their brows would bow their heads while praying and look skyward as they sang along. I remember my mother's finger on my leg, tapping time with the hymns while she sang along in her tiny soprano.

I recalled the exalted words from that humble man of long ago who preached peace.

All wound up together, it set quite a fable for a gullible little boy.

I sighed and looked around, pricked up my ears to find the long-stilled sounds. Where did everybody go? How did I get elected to be the last one in the church?

I thought of Alana. When I'd fallen from the building, it was so peaceful to be inside her. How wonderful it would be to feel like that all the time. It would have been wonderful if she could have stayed. But like she said, maybe Earth people have to struggle to find that kind of peace.

I had loved Alana. I had been through fire with her, literally. And through her, I had gained a little perspective with Sal, with my daughter, and with Cindy. But I'd known she didn't belong here. I was lucky to have known her briefly. The candle that burns brightest burns out the fastest. And Alana wasn't a candle. She was a blowtorch.

The door creaked open. My dad shuffled toward the altar, shoulders bent and head down. Neither of us spoke as he slowly made his way down the aisle and sat a few feet to my left. His breath came out in hurried wheezes. He took his handkerchief from his pocket and wiped the sweat off of his face. He took a moment to slow his breathing. "I heard you had another rough night."

"It was a son-of-a-bitch," I said.

He chuckled. "I guess I ain't the one to correct you for cussin' in my church."

"You better not," I said.

He scanned the room slowly. "You know, you look at things differently when you get to my age. I mean, this here is my life's work. I thought I had built up something important. But looking at it from here, sometimes I can hardly see the point of it at all."

"There were some good times," I said.

"That there were. I got to preach the Lord's words, I got to see you and your sisters grow up, I got to share it with your mom." His voice trailed off.

"Sam, I gotta get this off my chest. I was sure that I would precede you into the arms of Jesus, but now I see that ain't necessarily the case if He decides otherwise. So I got to come clean to you." He swallowed hard. "I done you wrong, son."

"Oh?"

"First off, I never should have treated that young white girl in such a disrespectful way. No matter what you and her had done. That wasn't Christian of me."

"Thanks, Dad."

"You figure on bringing her back? She's a right fine specimen of a woman."

"You were talking about acting in an unchristian manner."

"Oh, sure. Anyways, I have come to regret the way that I behaved over the years. It occurred to me that I had sought forgiveness from the Lord and from your mother, but I never thought of seeking forgiveness from you. Many times I broke faith with Jesus, and I know that it hurt you." He turned to face me. His eyes were misty.

"Dad ...."

"Forgive me, Sam."

I let out a little smile. "I don't think I'm qualified to hear a confession."

"Just say yes, damn you."

"Of course, Dad."

He looked up to the cross over the altar. "What have I got now, Sam, now that I'm so close to the end? My two daughters left town to go their own way. At least I still got my granddaughter. And I got you. I want us to be family. And damn if I almost didn't lose the two of you last night."

He looked down at his lap. His lower lip pursed. His body looked like a bag of bones with clothes hanging on it.

"It's okay, Dad."

"Any chance of you and my granddaughter's momma getting back together?"

"Cindy's not interested."

"Well, you make sure you do right by them, hear?"

I nodded.

He reached into his jacket and pulled out a yellow legal envelope. I took it, removed the letter, and saw his signature on the bottom of the power of attorney.

"I trust you, son."

I returned the letter to the folder and set it to the side.

"Did I ever tell you about Marvin Billings?" he said.

"Never heard of him."

"Well, he's a preacher just up from Mobile. Had to move up here to take care of his parents. He's one of those younger types, barely sixty-five. But he was inquiring about getting a congregation started here. With our own church just sitting here and all."

"Aren't you too old for that?"

"Well, hear me out. He could do the bulk of the preaching and the socializing. I'd be what you call a deacon emeritus. Course, we'd need lots of help. The building is sound, but still could use a lot of fixin' up around the edges. Calls for someone who's strong, someone who's not afraid to swing a hammer."

"So you want me to provide the cheap labor?"

"Cheap? Naw." He laughed and slapped my knee. "I ain't got no money to pay you."

"How can I turn down an offer like that?"

***

Last order of business was to call the developers to tell them the church was not for sale. They screamed at me and threatened to follow through with eminent domain proceedings. I wished them good luck in trying to confiscate a working church from its parishioners.

And soon my dad and I would get butts back in those seats and return to the business of saving souls.

With that peaceful thought, I dropped into my bed and quickly fell asleep.

***

I felt warm and content at first. Then the old ghosts stirred, bubbling out of the shadows. They called out from lonely alleys and seeped like pus from the edges of unhealed wounds. These were the feelings I hadn't felt since I started spending my nights with Alana, feelings I thought I had paid the price for so that they would leave me alone forever. But here they were, an indivisible part of me. Nagging me. Urging me. Making me a monster of discontent. I didn't want to listen, but I swear they told me to find the next girl, to do the next drug. They insisted I would ever be a lost, lonely soul who would never belong.

I sat up suddenly and reached down to rub the cramp in my hamstring. I was soaked in sweat and my underwear stuck to me. My intestines felt like they were tied in knots. I jumped out of bed, flicked on the light, and paced the floor. I found myself standing over the end table, opening the drawer, and pulling out the cigar box. I studied my choices. A bag of dope. A vial of cocaine. A bottle with some little red pills guaranteed to knock me out.

The box shook in my hands. It wasn't supposed to be like this. Alana promised me. She said everything was going to be all right.

It was all a joke, wasn't it? Whenever I saw a little daylight, there would be something horrible waiting for me. If it weren't my fire truck flipping over, it would be something else.

Alana was safe and sound. By now she was deeply involved in saving her world. Everybody'd gotten what they wanted, and I'd risked everything for it. Now there was nothing left over for me.

Go ahead, I told myself. Make yourself numb.

How could I help my father around the church? I thought of him telling me to paint this, to straighten that. I imagined the snarl of the old preacher's face. There was no way I could put up with that.

I shook my head to clear those thoughts. I was losing everything I'd gained in the last few days. I trembled. Maybe I needed something more. I still knew where to get the good stuff. I just had to make a call.

I threw the box and it smashed against the wall. I looked up to the ceiling as if I could see through the sky and into the stars. My body shook and I started sobbing hard. I fell on the bed and buried my face in the pillow, afraid that there was even a remote chance that anybody could see Sam Carver fall apart.

***

A persistent knock on the door woke me. I fought to focus, pushed myself up, and wiped my hand over my face. The clock said six-oh-seven. I threw on my robe and stomped through the house to the front door. This better not be Willie all drunk and crying, telling me how much he loved me.

"Coming," I barked. I undid the latch and shoved open the door.

Cindy stooped in the dark hall, her hands folding nervously over each other at her waist. "Hi, Sam."

She scrunched up her lips in what was supposed to be a smile, but I could tell she didn't mean it.

"It's six in the morning," I blurted out.

"I'm sorry, Sam. Maybe I should come back another time." She turned to walk down the stairs.

I grabbed her arm. "Wait. It's okay. What do you want?"

She stepped back up to the landing. "Do you think I could come in for a few minutes? There's something I've got to say."

***

We sat side by side on the couch. She leaned forward, her hands on her knees. I guess I never saw Cindy as frail, but now she looked like she'd crack into pieces at the slightest bump. I'd always wanted to see some vulnerability in her. She'd always been the strong one who took the high road and looked down on me as I messed up my life.

"Can I get you something? Tea? I think I got some instant coffee in the back of the cupboard."

She shook her head.

"Where's Rae?"

"My mother's watching her."

Her hands trembled. I touched her shoulder. "Is everything all right?"

She slid away from me. "Don't. Give me a chance. I got to tell you something, Sam. I need you to just sit there and listen."

I swallowed. I didn't think I could take a lecture.

She looked at her nails, scanned the water-stained walls of my apartment, which I knew were not that interesting. "Last night, I was so worried."

"I'm sorry about that," I said.

"You don't understand, Sam. Yes, I was worried sick about Rae. But I worried for you, too. Since your accident, every time I hear a siren I pray that you'll stay safe. When it's morning and I hear a knock on the door, I always think of that day."

"That was one kick-ass morning."

"I can still hear that knock. I remember opening the door and there was the chief with his hat in his hands, stuttering, trying to explain to me that you'd been in a terrible accident. I almost fainted and he had to grab my elbow. I thought of Rae without a father. I was still a girl myself. Things had been looking a little better for us, but when he told me, I just knew everything was going to be screwed up after that."

"Things did get screwed up," I said. You left me, I wanted to tell her. But I bit my lip.

"I've been thinking recently. I mean, everything might have been different if you were an accountant, if you worked at a repair garage. There's lots of other civil service jobs you could have gotten into. Jobs where you would have come home every night, where I wouldn't have had to worry."

"I don't think I'm cut out for the Parks Department."

She nodded. "You know, I was angry about that for a long time. I mean, why couldn't you do it for us? Come home safe and sound, help me put Rae to bed, watch the Late Show together on the couch. When you tried to save that little boy, I guess I started thinking a little differently. Oh, my God, he was Rae's age."

Cindy looked up to the ceiling and sighed. "I remember when we first went out. You were so handsome. You still are. I knew we were different types of people. But I guess I got carried away."

I wanted to tell her that I'd loved her from the first time I saw her, that we fit together like pieces of a puzzle. The things I needed she had, and vice versa. But time for that kind of talk was long gone.

"You looked so good when you graduated from the academy. All shiny and dressed in blue. I was so proud of you."

"Cindy, what's the point of this?"

"Sam, I need you to let me finish. When I'm done ,you may hate me. You may want to kick me out. But I have to tell you."

I nodded.

"Last night after I got Rae to bed, I was sitting in the kitchen with a cup of tea, looking out the back window, just thinking things through. It was such a beautiful night. I don't usually do something like this, but I put on my robe and slippers and went out onto the grass. You know my yard, it's not that big and there's a power line that runs through the back. But the stars just seemed really, really bright. So I'm watching them, and I can't help it but I realized I was smiling. You know, that's not really me, the type to sit and admire the scenery. But I did it last night. It just made me feel peaceful. So I'm watching and my eyes are locked on this one star. The star got bigger, you know, like it was falling down on me. But I wasn't afraid. The star kept falling and then it was hovering over the yard and I realized the star was green—no, more like liquid emeralds. I felt so peaceful and I thought I was looking right up into an angel. Do you believe in angels?"

I grabbed a fistful of cushion to steady myself. "I think I do."

"I know this sounds crazy. The angel started talking to me. I mean, not in words but in my head. It told me about you. And suddenly I felt really ashamed of myself." She looked over to me. She was weeping.

I don't think I'd ever seen Cindy cry before. Tears rolled down her perfect bronze skin and off her chin. Her root beer eyes glistened. Her lips looked swollen, and it took a lot of self-control not to grab her and kiss her.

"Tell me all of it," I said.

"The angel told me that you needed me. It told me that it knew for a fact that you still loved me with all your heart. It told me you were a good man, a special person who might mess up with a lot of things but when there was something important to be done, then you were a hero. And that sometimes a hero needs somebody behind him. Somebody to fill in the gaps in his life so he can go on being a hero. The angel said it knew that I loved you, too, and that it was up to me to make everything right."

"It said all that?"

"So what do you think I did? Crazy me, I called my mom to come watch Rae. I threw on my clothes and drove over here."

She turned to me, forcing herself to look into my eyes. "Sam Carver, I'd like us to be together again. I promise to stand by your side no matter how many bad things come our way. I want Rae to have brothers and sisters and I want you and me to make them together. Please, Sam? Please give me another chance?"

I don't think I could have stopped myself if I tried. I grabbed her shoulders and kissed her lips, her eyes, kissed the tears rolling down her cheeks. I ran my fingers over her hair as if she were something precious. Because she was.

A terrible weight lifted off of me. I felt whole. I didn't know how long the feeling would last. I hoped it would last forever.

Of course, life isn't a comic book. It's going to be filled with stuff like my wife changing the station while I'm watching the NCAA finals, my daughter spilling orange juice on my paycheck, our brand-new kitten peeing on my loafers, or my dad calling in the middle of the night because he's confused that he can't find my mom. There will be plenty of temptations like a sassy sister who struts by the firehouse and shakes her booty, or some old bud from college I ran into who invites me to his crib to get high.

Sometimes being a hero is acting the right way over stuff like that and a whole bunch more. By comparison, firefighting is a breeze.

But I'm going to try. For Cindy and Rae. And for me.

I'm going to try.

About the Author

 Jim Miner was born in Buffalo, New York. At an early age he perused the volumes of his parent's library and that piqued a lifelong fascination with books. When his peers were contemplating which college to go to, Jim decided to dive headfirst into life. He worked on docks, drove cab, flipped pizzas and slung hash, sailed the seas as a merchant seaman, crisscrossed the American highways, and finally settled into an action-filled career in the Buffalo Fire Department.

After thirty-one years, Jim attained the highest rank in the department: Division Chief. He retired due to on-the-job injuries. Unable to continue with the physically challenging lifestyle that he loved, Jim dove into his other passion: books.

Jim believes books to be the gateway to our culture and understanding of human nature. His mission is to inspire through his writing.

Made in the USA
Monee, IL
04 September 2021